Skylark

Jack O'Connell
Seattle
9 August 1996

OTHER TITLES IN THIS SERIES
(General Editor: Timothy Garton Ash)

Prague Tales
Jan Neruda

Be Faithful Unto Death
Zsigmond Móricz

IN PREPARATION

The Doll
Bolesław Prus

Skylark

Dezső Kosztolányi

Translated by Richard Aczel
Introduction by Péter Esterházy

⁺CEU

CENTRAL EUROPEAN UNIVERSITY PRESS

Budapest   London   New York

This edition first published in 1993 by Chatto & Windus Limited

Reissued in 1996 by
Central European University Press
1051 Budapest
Nádor utca 9

First published in Hungarian as *Pacsirta* in 1924

Distributed by
Oxford University Press, Walton Street, Oxford OX2 6DP
Oxford New York Athens Auckland Bangkok Bombay Toronto
Calcutta Cape Town Dar es Salaam Delhi Florence Hong Kong
Istanbul Karachi Kuala Lumpur Madras Madrid Melbourne
Mexico City Nairobi Paris Singapore Taipei Tokyo Toronto
and associated companies in Berlin Ibadan
Distributed in the United States
by Oxford University Press Inc., New York

English translation copyright © Richard Aczel 1993
Introduction copyright © Péter Esterházy 1993

British Library Cataloguing in Publication Data
A CIP catalogue record for this book is available from the British Library

ISBN 1 85866 059 9

Library of Congress Cataloging in Publication Data
A CIP catalog record for this book is available from the Library of Congress

Printed and bound in Great Britain by Biddles of Guildford, Surrey

Contents

Introduction

Everyone was born at that time: Joyce, Musil, Broch, Rilke, Thomas Mann, Kafka, Einstein, Picasso, Wittgenstein. They were all there in their respective cradles, everyone who counted, *le tout Paris*. The Hungarian modern classics were there too: Endre Ady, Mihály Babits, Gyula Krúdy, Zsigmond Móricz, Lajos Kassák, Béla Bartók, Zoltán Kodály.

Everything came together rather nicely at the turn of the century, before the world collapsed. A spiritual golden age, in which one of the most important and glittering actors was Dezső Kosztolányi.

He was born in Szabadka (Subotica)[1] in 1885, in that (to use his words) poor, grey, boring, dusty, bored, comical, provincial town. Even if we don't believe literature to be a mirror, in which reality catches a terror-stricken glimpse of itself, we can still admit that whoever reads *Skylark* (and also *The Golden Kite*) can recognise in Sárszeg the Szabadka of the *fin de siècle*. The years of the *fin de siècle* are years of progress, of industrialisation; it is then that Budapest is born and at once becomes a genuine big city – even a little bigger than it really is.

Szabadka is an in-between city, neither one thing

nor the other, frightfully respectable, its development well balanced, not as impetuous as, say, the more southerly Újvidék (Novi Sad), but not motionless either, like the more northerly Danubian town Baja. A similar indeterminacy can be felt in its bourgeoisie too; that is, the so-called gentlemanly middle class whose ambiguities we can see close up in *Skylark*. For this bourgeoisie considers itself heir both to the anti-Habsburg revolution of 1848 and to the *Ausgleich* of 1867, the compromise with Habsburg Austria, the birth of Kakania.[2]

Kosztolányi is a sparkling youth, as talented as the sun. He is thrown out of the school where his father is headmaster, perhaps in the spirit of the above-mentioned ambiguities, but more likely because of an argument about rhyme in the school literary debating society, where he refused to accept the authority of his teachers. His cousin is Géza Csáth, whose short prose pieces are in fact the first modern texts, the first writings that are really of this century.[3]

Kosztolányi arrives at the University of Budapest where he gets to know, among others, the poets Mihály Babits and Gyula Juhász. The correspondence of the three young men is touchingly beautiful, slap-dash, pompous, charming, sensitive, far-sighted and ambitious. Kosztolányi gets a taste of the city and immediately falls in love with it. He is one of the most steadfast, faithful lovers of Budapest. A good lover. For a short time he studies in Vienna, but gives it up, and at the age of twenty-three becomes a journalist for a Budapest daily, replacing the poet Endre Ady who is in Paris. He never breaks with journalism throughout his life. Generations have (or haven't) learned from him how to write a little two- or three-page feature.

He begins his literary career with poems and symbolic short stories. The first volume of poems to bring nationwide success is *The Complaints of a Poor Little Child*, which appears in 1910. After this he publishes a book nearly every year. Kosztolányi wants everything: life, literature, success.

In 1908 the journal *Nyugat* (West) had been founded, the alpha and omega of modern Hungarian literature. Even today the voices of our older literary colleagues still falter when they speak about an exceptional experience, like being booted out by the fearsome editor, Ernő Osvát. (No such great things awaited Hungarian writers of the next generation: we were booted out by absolute nonentities.)

Nyugat was a real periodical; that is, not merely a rallying point for first-rate writers, but a point of crystallisation and a force of integration in what might be called the new, modern movement. If we wish to attach labels we can say that Kosztolányi was a member of the first *Nyugat* generation, a representative of *l'art pour l'art*, a writerly writer; *Homo aestheticus*, as he called himself, in opposition to the *Homo moralis*. Courageously and coquettishly he chooses the 'babbling surface' as opposed to the 'silent depths'. 'Oh, sacred, clowning emptiness!' he cries out, in his 'Song of Kornél Esti', above all to his friend, the morally serious Babits, who grew more critical of Kosztolányi in later years.

Kosztolányi does not seek his own authentic face, but the authentic mask. He continually lives through roles and is close to classical decadence. The dandy is the last flowering of heroism in our age of decline, says the great dandyologist Baudelaire. Kosztolányi is a classical dandy, strict and severe.

He is multicoloured and ineffable, like a rainbow. There is nothing accidental about his shifting between genres. Critics at times heatedly debate whether he was primarily a poet or a prose writer, and whether his many-sidedness was an advantage or a disadvantage. I think it was neither the one nor the other, but simply a fact. In poetry he is the virtuoso, the child dizzied and shaken by all the wonders of the world. In prose he is precise, at times already an anxious anticipator of the *nouveau roman*, an adult facing up to the facts of the world.

He writes longer prose pieces from 1920. For him the twenties are the years of the novel: *Nero, the Bloody Poet, Skylark, The Golden Kite, Anna Édes.*[4] In 1924 he publishes a volume of verse entitled *The Complaints of the Sad Man*, rhyming with, answering and continuing the successful volume of 1910. This is a time of arrival. His reputation grows both at home and abroad. He becomes acquainted with Thomas Mann, who – as Hungarians never fail proudly to point out – writes a preface to the German edition of *Nero*.

Hungary has always had a great tradition in literary translation (the attentiveness of small nations – to themselves). Kosztolányi's achievement in this field is significant, his utterly exceptional sense of form almost predestines him for this. His translations include *A Winter's Tale* and *Alice in Wonderland*, to mention only two of the English references.

At the end of his life the virtuoso *Kornél Esti* stories appear, and the great late poems of the volume *Reckoning*. The 'Meistersinger spun from the magic of poetic play and fate, imagination and tears' dies a difficult death from cancer of the larynx in 1936.

A parlament a falra ment (Parliament hall has gone to the wall). First of all, of course, my poor translator goes to the wall, indeed, bangs his head against it, tearing out his hair. But such is life: hard. My life is hard, so was poor Kosztolányi's, why should the translator be the one to get off lightly? Yet even irrespective of the meaning of this sentence (that parliament hall has gone to the wall), one can appreciate its manifold beauty, rhyme and symmetry. This sentence formed the foundation of my children's political education. The Hungarian parliament, that unbelievable and – to Hungarian eyes – beautiful, if arguably intolerable, pseudo-Gothic building, at once announces the age of the young Kosztolányi, the incomprehensible self-confidence and ambition of the beginning of the century and the undeniable emptiness of its intentions. Driving past this building, all I had to do was point and the children would merrily whoop, 'Parliament hall has gone to the wall.' In those days, anything more about the Hungarian parliament, or our so-called socialist democracy, simply wasn't worth knowing.

Kosztolányi was perhaps the world's greatest

rhymer, or master of rhyme. The Hungarian language is particularly well suited to this circus stunt, indeed it is hardly even a matter of bravado. Hungarian, unlike other languages, to this day treats rhyme, that cheap and dubious element, as a generally accepted and usable possibility.

I would even venture to say that it was Kosztolányi who did most to make the Hungarian language what it is today. To change a language visibly, perceptibly, at the everyday level, is something very few writers ever achieve. Kosztolányi changed the Hungarian sentence. The Hungarian language anyway stands in a dramatic relationship to the sentence. Our language, as Babits wrote, 'doesn't roll along on such well-worn wheels, doesn't think in place of the writer. It lacks those solid, ready-made phrases, those tiny components of style on which the English or French writer can draw without so much as thinking.' In Hungarian there are no clearly defined prohibitions; in a certain sense everything is possible and everything has to be invented over and over again. Every single sentence is an individual achievement. This individuality is both good and bad.

Kosztolányi simplified the Hungarian sentence, made it shorter, purer. The nineteenth-century sentence was long-winded, the meaning wandering through long periodic structures, and in any case the Hungarian long sentence is a dubious formation because the words do not have genders and the subordinate clauses are more uncertainly connected to the main clauses than in the reassuring rigour of a *Satzbau*

(German sentence construction). Such sentences totter along, uncertain even of themselves, stammer a little; in short, are extremely lovable.

These are our internal affairs, important internal affairs; let's look at what lies beyond the sentence.

First of all, in the spirit of Kosztolányi, we might say: nothing. Beyond language there is nothing. There are only words, and from these words the poet builds up everything, not just his books, his works, but ultimately he assembles himself and his own fate through words – his feelings, his father, his lovers. This is, of course, an exaggeration, even if it happens to be true. It is true because a writer – in the opinion of this present writer – should not have something to say, and an exaggeration because it would not be a good thing if his books didn't have anything to say either. If the writer speaks, that's pedantry; if the book keeps silent – then what's the point?

Kosztolányi's books, let's be precise here, speak about death, about play and about Kakania, or rather about the interweaving of all three, sometimes about their identity, about the confusion of twentieth-century man for whom life is a game, the whole world is a game, and this world is: death. But even this is not certain.

He writes in his diary:

> I have always really been interested in just one thing: death. Nothing else. I became a human being when, at the age of ten, I saw my grandfather dead, whom at that time I probably loved more than anyone else.

xiii

It is only since then that I have been a poet, an artist, a thinker. The vast difference which divides the living from the dead, the silence of death, made me realise that I had to do something. I began to write poetry. [. . .] For me, the only thing I have to say, however small an object I am able to grasp, is that I am dying. I have nothing but disdain for those writers who also have something else to say: about social problems, the relationship between men and women, the struggle between races, etc., etc. It sickens my stomach to think of their narrow-mindedness. What superficial work they do, poor things, and how proud they are of it.

Kosztolányi is stoical, but oddly so, one might even say insincerely so. His is the stoicism of a young man. Kosztolányi's every reflex is that of a young man. (He grew old hard, found it hard to grow old, like a beautiful woman.) He believed in nothing except style. Yet he wasn't a man of principle. He is characterised at once by a love of life and a terror of life. He has no magic potions, he says, nothing helps – but why should one be disappointed because of this? He raises the questions of a man of today, but not the questions of a disillusioned man. We hear the dignity, at times the desire to show off, of a man in the shadow of death.

He sets to work on *Skylark* in the spring of 1923. Szabadka already belongs to another country, our mothers and fathers belong to another country, they are just in the process of learning Serbian; everything is alien, once again our own past is disappearing.

Kosztolányi looks back at a world he knew well, where he knew his way around as if at home, but without nostalgia. He knows how the story ends; he sits there in his own nothingness.

The time of the novel is 1899, the eternal present moment, a Faustian moment: in miniature, in a provincial setting. Kosztolányi shows us the margins of a world whose centre we know from Musil. We are in the borderlands of Kakania.

Kosztolányi's character as a prose writer does not, however, stand close to that of Musil, rather to that of Chekhov. He shares that same helpless fascination for the banal and trivial, for a drama-of-being which can be unravelled from a remote gesture, a twitch of the mouth, a dismissive wave of the hand, from lamplight and ugliness. A spider's web over a mine.

Skylark's ugliness is not a symbol. This ugliness is the unnameable anxiety which we would dearly love to forget, to dispel, but it is not possible, it always comes back, is always with us, relentless, just like a daughter with her father. Skylark's hideousness, her soft puffiness, dullness, aggressive goodness is: us. It is our lives that are so stiff, so predictable, so impersonal, so Hungarian. Skylark is eternal. There's no deliverance. Our little bird always flies home.

Kosztolányi's prose is quiet and sharp. Today our books are noisier and perhaps more blurred.

Péter Esterházy
1993

I

---

*in which the reader is introduced to an elderly couple
and their daughter, the apple of their eye, and hears
of complicated preparations for a trip to the plains*

The dining-room sofa was strewn with strands
of red, white and green cord, clippings of packing twine, shreds of wrapping paper and the
scattered, crumpled pages of the local daily, the same
fat letters at the top of each page: *Sárszeg Gazette,
1899.*

Beside the mirror on the wall, in a pool of bright
sunlight, a calendar showed the day and the month:
Friday 1 September.

And through the window of an elaborately carved
wooden case, the sauntering brass hands of a grandfather clock, which sliced the seemingly endless day
into tiny pieces, showed the time: half past twelve.

Mother and Father were busy packing.

They were wrestling with a worn, brown leather
suitcase. When they had squeezed one last comb into

the canvas pocket of the partition, they zipped it shut and lowered it to the floor.

There it stood, ready for the road, bursting at the seams, its bloated belly protruding on either side like that of a cat about to bear nine kittens.

The remaining bits and pieces they packed into a wicker travel basket: lace knickers, a blouse, a pair of felt slippers, a buttonhook and other oddments their daughter had carefully set aside.

'The toothbrush,' said Father.

'Heavens, the toothbrush!' nodded Mother. 'We nearly forgot her toothbrush.'

Still shaking her head, she hurried out into the hall and from there to her daughter's room to fetch the toothbrush from the enamelled tin washbasin.

Father pressed down once more on his daughter's belongings, gently stroking them flat and smooth with his palm.

It was not the first time that his brother-in-law, Béla Bozsó, had invited them to spend the summer in Tarkő, to take a well-earned rest on his little plot.

His three-roomed 'castle' stood among ramshackle farm buildings in the middle of a small plain, no more than 150 acres wide. And well they remembered the spacious guest room in the outer wing, its white-washed walls hung with hunting rifles and antlers.

They hadn't visited for years, but Mother would often speak of her brother's 'estate' and the little reedy brook that hid at the foot of the hill, where, as a child, she had launched her paper boats.

They kept postponing the trip.

But this year, every letter that arrived from the plain closed with the same entreaty: come and see us at last, come as soon as you can.

In May they had finally made up their minds to go. But summer came and went as usual, with preparations for winter, the cooking of preserves, the bottling of apples, pears and cherries.

By the end of August they wrote to say it was too late again. They were still stuck at home, too old to feel like moving. But they'd send their daughter instead. Just for a week. She worked so hard, a break would do her good.

Their relatives were overjoyed with the news.

The postman called every day. Uncle Béla wrote to the girl and so did his wife, Aunt Etelka. The girl wrote back, Mother wrote to her sister-in-law, Father to his brother-in-law, asking him to be sure to wait at the station in person with his chaise, for the farmstead was a good three-quarters of an hour on foot. Everything was agreed.

Yet even in the last couple of days the telegrams went on crossing, clearing up the minutest of details. Now there was no going back.

Mother returned with the toothbrush. Father wrapped it carefully in tissue paper.

They made one last inspection of the room, then, satisfied that nothing had been overlooked, they pressed the lid down on the wicker basket.

But the key refused to turn and the lock kept springing open. Finally, they tied the basket shut with packing twine, father bearing down upon the lid with his hollow chest, the veins bulging on his forehead.

They had all risen with the dawn that day, setting about the task of packing at once, bustling to and fro in their unaccustomed excitement. They had hardly even stopped for lunch; one thing or another would always come to mind.

Now everything was ready.

They set the wicker basket down on the floor beside the suitcase. A luggage trolley rattled over the paved courtyard path that led all the way from Petőfi Street, across the garden and right up to the veranda.

A gangling youth strolled in and threw suitcase and basket indifferently on to the trolley before wheeling it out again and heading off towards the railway station.

Father wore a mouse-grey suit, the exact colour of his hair. Even his moustache was the same light shade of grey. Large bags of crumpled, worn, dry skin hung beneath his eyes.

Mother, as always, wore black. Her hair, which she slicked down with walnut oil, was not yet altogether white, and her face showed hardly a wrinkle. Only along her forehead ran two deep furrows.

Yet how alike they looked! The same trembling, startled light in their eyes, their gristly noses narrowing to the same fine point and their ears tinted with the same red glow.

They glanced at the grandfather clock. Father checked his pocket watch, which was a little more reliable. They went out on the veranda and called in unison:

'Skylark!'

A girl sat on a bench by the flowerbeds, beneath the horse-chestnut tree. She was crocheting a tablecloth from a ball of yellow cotton.

Only her black hair could be seen, casting – like the leaves of the horse-chestnut tree upon the ground below – a heavy shadow on about two-thirds of her face.

She did not move at once. Perhaps she hadn't heard.

In any case, she liked to sit like this, head bowed, peering at her work even when she had tired of it. The experience of many long years had taught her that this posture suited her best.

Perhaps she heard some sound, but still did not look up. She governed herself with all the discipline of an invalid.

This time they called louder:

'Skylark!'

Then louder still:

'*Skylark!*'

The girl raised her eyes to the veranda, where, on the top step, her mother and father stood waiting.

They had given her that name years ago, Skylark, many, many years ago, when she still sang. Somehow the name had stuck, and she still wore it like an outgrown childhood dress.

Skylark breathed a deep sigh – she always sighed thus deeply – wound up her ball of yellow cotton, dropped it in her work basket and set off towards the little arbour overgrown with vine leaves. So it was time, she thought; the train would soon be leaving;

5

tonight she'd be sleeping at her uncle's on the Tarkő plain. She waddled along a little like a duck.

The elderly couple watched with fond smiles as she drew near. Then, when her face finally revealed itself between the leaves, the smiles paled slightly on their lips.

'It's time to go, my dear,' said Father, looking at the ground.

II

in which we walk the length of Széchenyi Street to
the railway station and the train pulls out at last

They passed beneath the row of poplars lining
Sárszeg's only tarmacked street, Széchenyi
Street, running in one straight line to the railway station. They might just have been taking one of
their daily walks: Mother to the right, Father to the left
and Skylark in between.

Mother talked about how she had packed the toothbrush only at the last minute, and explained where she
had put this and that. Father carried a white striped
woollen blanket and a flask he had filled with good
well-water from home, for the journey.

Ákos Vajkay said nothing. He tramped along in
silence, looking at his daughter.

She wore an enormous hat with outmoded dark-
green feathers, a light dress and, to protect herself
from the scorching sun, opened a pink parasol which
sifted shards of light across her face.

Skylark was a good girl, Ákos would often say, to

7

himself as much as anyone else. A very good girl, his only pride and joy.

He knew she was not pretty, poor thing, and for a long time this had cut him to the quick. Later he began to see her less clearly, her image gradually blurring in a dull and numbing fog. Without really thinking any more, he loved her as she was, loved her boundlessly.

Five, ten years must have passed since he had abandoned all hope of one day giving Skylark. away in marriage. The idea no longer even crossed his mind. Yet whatever happened to the girl affected him profoundly. Even if she simply changed her hairstyle, or put on a winter coat at the end of autumn or a new dress for the spring, he could be miserable for weeks before he grew accustomed to her altered appearance.

And Ákos was miserable now. He pitied his daughter, and took his pity out on himself. He watched her intently, almost offensively, still unable to get used to her face, at once both plump and drawn, the pudgy nose, the flared, horsy nostrils, the severe, masculine eyebrows and the tiny watery eyes which somehow reminded him of his own.

He had never really understood women, but knew only too well that his daughter was ugly. And not just ugly any more, but withered and old. A veritable old maid.

It was only in the flood of almost theatrically rosy sunlight cast by the parasol that this became irrevocably clear to him. A caterpillar under a rosebush, he thought to himself.

He ambled along in his mouse-grey suit until they

reached Széchenyi Square, the only square, the only *agora*, in Sárszeg, where instinctively he strode a couple of paces ahead, so as not to have to walk beside her.

Here stood the Town Hall, the Baross Café, the old grammar school with its worn and hollowed stone steps, its little wooden tower whose bell would chime each morning, calling the children to school; here was the King of Hungary restaurant and, across the square, the Széchenyi Inn, backing on to the Kisfaludy Theatre and offering a slanting view of a one-storey palace, decorated with climbing roses and a bright gold lightning conductor, one of the finest buildings in the town, and home of the Gentlemen's Club. Further down began the shops: the paint shop, two ironmongers, Vajna's stationery and bookshop, the St Mary Pharmacy and a new, smartly furnished leathergoods store, Weisz and Partner. The owner stood smoking a cigar in the doorway, bathing his cheerful watermelon face in the sun. Removing the cigar from his mouth, he bowed and greeted the Vajkays with a broad grin.

Ákos, like the rest of his family, rarely ventured into town. The gaping openness and never-ending curiosity made him feel awkward.

Sitting on the terrace sipping beer, the afternoon clientele of the Széchenyi Café looked up from their newspapers and stared at Skylark. Not disrespectfully, just the way they always did: with a look of grey, benevolent sympathy, lined in red with a certain malevolent pleasure.

With this the old man put a stop to his sullen, self-tormenting thoughts. He slowed his step, allowing his daughter to draw level, then marched beside her defiantly, so that he too should face the sympathy and malevolent pleasure. And as always at such times, he tugged nervously at his left shoulder, pulling it close, as if to cloak his embarrassment at the offence his own flesh and blood had caused to the order of nature.

They arrived at the railway station. The local train was already puffing and fuming on the track like a little coffee grinder. The bell sounded for all aboard.

They bustled along the platform towards the ladies' carriage, hoping to find a suitable seat for Skylark. But to their dismay, there was not a single place unoccupied. Skylark had to stagger from one crowded carriage to the next before finding a second-class compartment at the end of the train, occupied by a young man and an old, gaunt Catholic priest. They decided this would have to do and Father climbed aboard to arrange the luggage.

Ákos swung the suitcase on to the train and lifted the wicker basket up to the luggage rack all by himself. He handed his daughter the white striped woollen blanket, then the water flask so that she shouldn't drink strange water during the journey. He drew the curtains so that she shouldn't fry in the burning sun, and even bounced up and down on her seat to try the springs. Then he bade his daughter farewell, kissing her on both cheeks. He never kissed her on the lips.

He climbed down from the train. Pulling his black bowler hat over his eyebrows, he joined his wife, who stood waiting beside the carriage anxiously watching the window. And yes, disguise it as they might, Mother and Father were already crying. Quiet, unaffected tears, but tears all the same.

The good citizens of Sárszeg who watched them with their curious, provincial, peering eyes, could hardly have been surprised.

They had long grown accustomed to the Vajkays crying in public. They cried every Sunday in church, at Mass, during the sermon, they cried at funerals, at weddings, at national celebrations, when all the solemn flags and speeches raised their spirits to a higher plane. It was almost as if they cherished such occasions.

At home they lived quite cheerfully. But whenever an opportunity presented itself, some pretext for being generally moved, they'd 'have a good cry' as they'd say to each other later, smiling slightly, still wiping the tears from their eyes.

And now they were crying again.

When she had finished arranging her belongings in the compartment, Skylark went over to the window. She noticed at once the tears in her parents' eyes, but tried to force an expression of indifference, even a little smile. She didn't dare speak, for fear her voice might abandon her midway.

Their parting was long and awkward. It seemed as if the train would never depart. Local trains are always somehow overzealous. At first they panic everyone into believing they are just about to thunder off down the track with an almighty jolt, then, at the very last minute, there is always some improbable hitch. They had plenty of time for their farewells and were beginning to run out of things to say. The couple dried their tears and lingered awkwardly on the platform, longing for the protracted episode to come to an end.

'Don't catch cold now,' said Mother fussily, 'in this infernal heat.'

'There's water in the flask,' Father added. 'You won't go drinking cold water, will you?'

'And no melon. Or cucumber salad either. For heaven's sake, Skylark, don't let them give you cucumber salad.'

The train let out a terror-stricken whistle which gave all three of them a start. But still it did not set off.

'Well, God bless,' said Ákos, drawing together his remaining strength and bringing the conversation to a close in a decisive, manly fashion. 'God bless, and take care, my child.'

'Skylark,' cried Mother, chewing the end of her handkerchief because she was about to start crying again, 'my dear girl, you'll be gone ages.'

Only now did Skylark speak.

'Friday. I'll be back on Friday. A week today.'

And at that moment the ramshackle engine gave its short, flat carriages an unexpected jolt, and set off lisping and spluttering down the track.

It rattled out into the open fields.

The girl leaned out of the window. She gazed back at her parents, standing on the platform side by side, waving their little handkerchiefs, yet somehow stiff as statues. For a while she could still see them. Then they disappeared from view.

Barracks, towers and haystacks waltzed, pillars raced, lilac bushes swayed to and fro in the wind whipped up by the train. Dust and sunlight stung her eyes and she coughed from the smoke of burning coal. Everything reeled about her head.

Skylark was much like her father. She simply lived her life from day to day. But now, as the receding landscape, the alternating meadows made her think of what could never change, would always stay the same, her heart sank.

She walked to another window which was still shut. But here in the glass she could see her own face. She didn't believe in looking at herself; it was a sign of vanity, they said, and, besides, what was the point?

She set off back down the swaying corridor of the train, hurrying anxiously as if in flight, as if in search of a more secure and secluded space in which to hide her pain.

When she reached the compartment where the young man and the old, gaunt Catholic priest sat in silence, she tried to return to her seat. But now she could no longer contain her suffering.

Her eyes filled with tears.

Her first feeling must have been one of alarm, for she suddenly raised a hand to her eyes as if to avert suspicion and to deceive her fellow passengers, surprised and horrified to find that what she had feared most of all, had counted on coming only later – when she arrived on the plain perhaps, or later still – had already begun. So many tears. In all the world she had never thought there could be so many tears.

She didn't reach for her handkerchief. It would have been to no avail. She wept openly in front of the two men, still on her feet, flaunting her torment almost indecently, heaving her interminable curse with a mixture of indifference and ostentation. A thick membrane of fathomless tears clouded her eyes. She saw no one, and didn't care who saw her.

Then all her nerves and muscles began to jerk and twitch, convulsions seized her throat, rasping and scratching like some unbearably bitter poison chasing down a mouthful of sweet wine.

The two men witnessed in silence the timeless process of weeping. Lungs billowing with a single sigh, twitching lips snatching desperately for air, a few more gasps and spasms, then the winding-down, which also hurt, even if it signalled the death of pain.

Skylark leaned back against the door of the compartment to spread the heavy burden of her labour. There was hardly a grimace, hardly a sign of physical pain on her face. Only that flood of boiling tears flowing through the channels of her eyes, nose and mouth, shaking her otherwise unaffected body from the knees to the shoulder blades, a force invisible to anyone but her, the rising presence of a shapeless memory, a half-formed thought, an image of torment, no less acute for being inexpressible.

She sat down in her place. Her broad face warmed in the sunshine, stains of hot lymph making her nose glow red. In that feathered hat of hers, poor thing, she really did look quite grotesque.

The young man – a handsome but gormless sort – who had been reading until now, set his book down on his knees and stared at the quietly sobbing girl. An offer of assistance kept finding itself on the tip of his tongue, but never passed his lips. He simply couldn't imagine what had happened. Perhaps she had fallen ill, or suffered the kind of 'blow' they wrote about in the cheap paperback novels he read.

Skylark paid him no attention whatsoever. She stared resolutely, almost malevolently above his head. He was no different from all the other young men who avoided her gaze and registered her approach with the same spiteful, studied coldness. This was her only form of self-defence.

The boy understood this instinctively. He withdrew his inquisitive gaze and buried it in his book. Skylark changed places. She sat down facing the priest, who all this time behaved as if he had noticed nothing. He was reading from a breviary printed in red letters, resting his head against the inner window of the corridor. The protruding cheekbones of his somewhat sickly face betrayed a kind of inner peace.

He wore a threadbare cassock with a button missing and a crumpled celluloid collar. This slight, humble soldier of the cross, who had returned to his village to grow old, engulfed by love and goodness, knew exactly what was going on. But out of tact he said nothing, and out of sympathy showed not the slightest sign of interest. He knew the world was a vale of tears.

Only now did he cast a glance at the girl, his keen, blue eyes intense from regular encounters with the Lord; a steadfast glance that caused Skylark no offence, and almost seemed to cool her burning face. She looked back gratefully, as if to thank him for his kind attention.

She still had tears in her eyes, but no longer shook or sobbed. Before long she had completely calmed down. She gazed at the passing countryside and, from time to time, at the worn and haggard priest, who, past sixty and already nearing the grave, radiated a certain serene simplicity, reassuring and consoling her without words. Throughout the journey they did not speak at all.

Some thirty minutes later the young man got to his feet, slung his double-barrelled shotgun over his shoulder, picked up his hunting hat and left the compartment. Skylark nodded a silent goodbye.

At Tarkő the priest helped her down with her baggage. Uncle Béla stood waiting by his chaise, his friendly, dumpy face, discoloured by the healthy air of the plains, shining as he beckoned. As always, a cigarette burned between his teeth.

Skylark smiled. Her uncle's beard was yellow-red, just like the Persian tobacco he always smoked. His familial kiss reeked of the same tobacco.

And someone else was waiting for her, too. Tiger, the hunting dog. She ran alongside the chaise when they set off, and was still beside them when they reached the farmstead.

III

---

in which we learn a thing or two about Mother and Father's first day alone

Ákos Vajkay, formerly of Kisvajka and Kőrös-hegy, retired county archivist, and his wife Antónia Vajkay, née Bozsó, of Kecfalva, gazed after the train as it panted out of the station and dwindled to a smoky black dot on the horizon.

They stared dumbly into space like the speechless victims of some sudden loss, their eyes still hankering after the spot where they had last seen her. They couldn't bring themselves to walk away.

When people go away they vanish, turn to nothing, stop being. They live only in memories, haunting the imagination. We know they go on being somewhere else, but no longer see them, just as we no longer see those who have already passed away. Skylark had never left them like that before. At most she had been away for a day, when she travelled to Cegléd, or for half a day, on an excursion to Tarliget. And even then they had hardly been able to wait for her return. It was

17

very hard to imagine that she would not be coming home with them today.

Such thoughts tormented the elderly couple. They hung their heads and stared at the gravel on the track as mournfully as at an unexpectedly and hastily filled grave.

They could already feel their loneliness. Swelling painfully, it hovered around them in the silence the departing train had left behind.

A rangy railway official came towards them, wearing a red armband and the insignia of a winged wheel on his sleeve. He had been standing between the rails when the train pulled out and was now shuffling hesitantly towards the office.

His face was pale, but on his narrow brow, beneath the peak of his railway cap, his summer pimples bloomed brightly like ripe cherries. His uniform hung loosely about his chest.

He snorted and snuffled, continually plagued by colds. Even in this fine, sunny weather his left nostril was constantly blocked. To dignify his wheezing he would let out the odd sigh. He even coughed now and then, although he had no need to cough at all.

They spotted him at once. Géza Cifra.

The woman nudged her husband. Ákos had already seen him, but hadn't wanted to speak. They wondered what to do.

They turned away, not wanting to face the boy.

They had known Géza Cifra for some nine years.

In the days when he was first stationed in Sárszeg, he had often visited their home, where Ákos would receive him with his customary affability. They'd invite him to tea, sometimes even to dinner. Géza Cifra would accept their invitations; out of awkwardness, mainly, for he couldn't say no to anyone. He praised the tea and extolled the dinner. At the Catholic Ladies' Club ball he danced the second quadrille with Skylark. He took her out rowing with friends on the lake at Tarliget and was generally attentive to her – in so far as he knew how to be attentive to a woman. But then, without cause or foundation, rumours began to spread in town that he would ask for Skylark's hand. At this he suddenly began to stay away.

He got in with an altogether different crowd, a handful of junior clerks, shady office boys, well below even his social station although close to him in spirit. Consequently, he felt ashamed of his friends, rather as a man who knows he has married beneath himself might feel ashamed of his wife. They met secretly in their lodgings, scoffing at everything, disparaging everyone, especially one another. An amber-tipped cigarette holder or a silver cigarette case could fill them with such unspeakable envy, and the good fortune of one of their number with such loathing, that they would immediately conspire against him and (remaining within the bounds of friendship, of course) contemplate causing him fatal injury, denouncing him in an anonymous letter or simply wringing his neck.

Géza Cifra, who was not naturally inclined to such malevolence, occasionally felt disgusted by his companions. But not enough to break free of them, for, while they were held together in petty wickedness by the iron clasp of passion, he was bound to them through plain lack of cultivation. He simply enjoyed their schoolboy pranks and nasty jokes.

His friendship with the Vajkays gradually cooled. They would no more than exchange greetings and the odd polite word when, as now, their paths occasionally crossed.

Skylark never mentioned Géza Cifra. There had, after all, been others like him. Her parents, however, had never forgotten the boy. Géza Cifra was the one person in all the world they could never forgive and would never cease to resent. What sin, what crime had he committed? None, to be sure. He had never laid a finger on their daughter, never led her on or deceived her, never made improper suggestions as others had.

All that had happened, one fine March evening during the first year of their acquaintance some nine years before, was that Géza Cifra had bumped into Skylark in front of the King of Hungary restaurant and had, out of simple courtesy, escorted her as far as the Baross Café, talking on the way about the weather, good and bad, causing Skylark, to her parents' complete surprise, to arrive five minutes late for supper, which began, as custom had it, at approximately eight o'clock.

This the Vajkays could never forget. Years later they would still reflect on their daughter's mysterious evening promenade, and Géza Cifra became a kind of family legend, swelling inside them entirely unnourished by fact. At times they despised him, at times they accused him, and at times he was simply that spineless scoundrel, that shamefully unfeeling libertine, that wretched – if not altogether ill-intentioned – weakling of a young man, to whom between themselves they only ever referred as *him*. They never so much as uttered his name.

He had at one time undoubtedly met with the Vajkays' highest approval. They could never have wished their daughter a more appropriate suitor. They had always dreamed of a decent, homely type who'd wear unironed broadcloth trousers and a painfully knitted brow; who'd sweat a little and blush when he spoke.

Géza Cifra was just such a man.

He was always embarrassed and ill at ease. Uncomfortable in the company of people brighter than himself, he could not disguise his torment. It hurt to look at him.

He was terrified of everyone and everything. Terrified of arriving too early or of leaving too late; terrified of talking too much or too little, of eating too much or too little. At dinner he would always refuse something twice before accepting it the third time round, his head tilted to one side, wearing a sheepish smile. Even now he did not know what to do.

He could never have imagined what he meant to that poor old couple. All he could sense was that they were colder towards him now, and this he found quite natural. Should he approach them or not?

He was tempted above all to disappear without seeming to notice them. Indeed he resolved to do so at once. Then, thinking how impolite that might seem, how scandalous and ungrateful, he grew alarmed by his own intentions and changed his mind. In the end, he did what he always did in such situations: the opposite of what he'd initially intended.

He walked over to them.

When Géza Cifra raised a gloved hand to his cap and greeted them, Ákos, still standing firm beside his wife, felt a shiver run down his spine.

'Gone away?' asked Géza Cifra.

'Away,' Father echoed hoarsely.

At this point the conversation stalled. It was the moment Géza Cifra always dreaded.

'Actually,' he began, without knowing how to continue. With that and similar words he tried to stop the gaps in the conversation, but to no avail. He smiled, then grimaced. He shivered hot and cold, then swallowed hard. He thought he had tarried long enough, then decided that he hadn't and it would still be improper to withdraw. His Adam's apple slid up and down his goitrous throat.

He cast a flustered glance at his pocket watch.

'Two forty-seven,' he said, taking refuge in railway talk. 'Should get in at five twenty.'

Father made no reply, but Mother smiled. A warm, familiar smile, imploring him to stay, as it often had in times long since gone by.

'The train won't be late?' she inquired.

'No,' Géza Cifra replied.

Now he felt sure he could retire. He wanted to salute, but only managed a modest tip of the cap.

The elderly couple made their way out of the station.

A long afternoon lay before them, and, not knowing what else to do, they headed back to the house. They even hurried a little, as if something still awaited them at home.

Ákos had left the county administration some five years previously, taking early retirement on account of his illness. His days passed quietly, melting into months and years. Almost unawares, he had reached the age of fifty-nine. He looked a good deal older, sixty-five at least.

Before retiring he had bought the single-storey house on Petőfi Street from the remains of an inheritance left him by his maternal uncle, Gedeon Körcsy, together with the few odd pennies he had scraped together during his career. Apart from the house, he owned nothing else in the world. Here he would pace up and down, hands behind his back, growing weary of doing nothing. He'd wait for his wife and daughter to get up in the morning, then wait for them to go to bed in the evening. He waited for the table to be laid, then waited to see it cleared again. He pottered about restlessly with an anxious glow in his eyes.

He had not moved in society for years. He neither drank nor smoked. Not only his family doctor, Dr Gál, but also the professor he had consulted in Pest, had warned against arteriosclerosis and forbidden him from taking alcohol and – more distressingly – from smoking his beloved cigars.

The only passion remaining to him from the past

was to sit in his cramped and perpetually damp study, leafing through a volume of Iván Nagy's great tome on Hungarian noble families, or Géza Cseghe*ö*'s precious and thoroughly entertaining little book on the history of coats of arms. He knew a thing or two about heraldry and blazonry, archivology and sigillography, diplomatics and sphragistics. He'd sit and syllabise endless Latin letters of foundation – *litterae armales* – written by ancient kings, and never came across a single document, a single subpoenal *executionale* or capitulary *fassio*, on which he could not immediately shed some light. He saw at a glance how the various families branched out, and could at once divine the meaning of a horizontal bar in the panel of a crest, an eagle with spread wings, a solitary golden globe. And he loved his vocation dearly. The sheer delight of peering through the magnifying glass at a mouse bite, a moth hole or the zigzag channel carved by a woodworm, while breathing in the acerbic fragrance of the mould. It was here he came alive; here in the past. And as others travel miles to visit fortune-tellers, distinguished gentlemen from far-away counties had for many years made pilgrimages to Pet*ö*fi Street to discover their pasts.

In his younger days he had earned his living from the 'verification of lawful lineage', from *filiatio* and *deductio*, and although he no longer had any financial need of his vocation, he found himself unable to give it up. He could become as ensconced in a *donatio regia* as in some fascinating chess puzzle, and would dig through generations of ancestors and kinsmen, grandparents and great-grandparents, until he arrived at the most exciting of all, the primogenitor, the first fore-father, the *primus acquirens*, whose ingenuity had established the fortune of a whole generation and whose heroic deeds reflected glory on all who descended from him. His head hummed with King's Wardens, Dames of the Star Cross Order and Knights of the Maltese Cross. He had nothing but admiration for those admissible at court.

When he had no other work, he'd turn to his own friends and acquaintances. He had once even wanted to verify the lawful lineage of Géza Cifra. For a while the genealogical *tabella* progressed quite smoothly. He even took it with him to the archives of the neighbouring county in order to gather more recent data. Then he suddenly got stuck. Neither he nor the records could uncover the exact identity of Géza Cifra's paternal grandfather. And so the family tree he had begun to sketch remained unfinished. Its frondose branches withered as if ravaged by a violent storm. Whenever Ákos came upon this sketch among his other papers, a scornful smile flitted across his face. Géza Cifra was just a common upstart, and not of noble descent at all.

But oh, the stories he could tell about his own ancestors, whom he seemed to know more intimately than the living. The Ádám Vajkays and the Sámuel Vajkays who had lived in the mountains and kidnapped young girls. Or the women, the Kláras and Katalins and Erzsébets, who had taken part in Maria Theresa's powderpuff balls. Or his wife's ancestors, the powerful Bozsós who had lived as wealthy aristocrats with splendid estates right up until the middle of the eighteenth century; or even about the odd isolated word once uttered by ancient kinsmen in the depths of bygone centuries and about the obscure golden lily which blossomed on the scarlet panel of their crest. Such ancient blood throbbed in their veins that they hadn't even possessed a noble patent, acquiring their rank through donated estates and laying claim to their coat of arms by right of ancient custom. This one escutcheon hung in a frame on his study wall, together with a family tree he had painted himself in fine, pale watercolours, after decades of fastidious research had led him all the way back to King Endre II. His own humble position and meagre means prevented him from applying for the title of royal and imperial chamberlain, a title upon which, according to his ancestry, he could none the less make every lawful claim. But this never disturbed him in the least. Not a man of outward vanity, he was interested in the principle alone, in itself sufficient to swell his secret self-esteem.

By the time he reached fifty, his work had been complete. He had traced the lineage of every last Vajkay and Bozsó, dead or alive. What remained to be done? Browsing over sheets of paper, onionskin and parchment, he would sit in his study for hours on a creaky couch draped with a Turkish rug, rapidly losing its colour in the stuffy, museumlike air. Here he'd ruminate about the future.

But all the future seemed to hold for certain was the

prospect of his approaching death. Of this simple fact he would speak with all the callous indifference and alarming objectivity of an old man, often bringing his wife and daughter to the brink of tears. On the tomb of his long-departed parents he set a stone of dark-brown marble, engraved in gold lettering with the words: The Vajkay Family Vault. He took care of the grave, planted four box shrubs beside it and regularly watered the turf. He even painted the bench where he would sit and muse during his visits to the cemetery.

It was, he announced, his wish to be buried there when the time came, between his mother and father. He should be laid in state in the guest room, the hall should be draped in black and only two priests should perform the funeral. He kept his will in a sealed envelope locked in the bottom drawer of his writing desk, and informed his wife of where it might be found when the time arrived. The last years of his life he spent increasingly in preparation for his death.

The only time he'd betray any anxiety at all was when a member of his funeral society died. Then he'd hurry off to town with his funeral register – his 'little book', as he called it – to pay his society dues. Back at home he'd leaf once more through the register, checking that the fee had been duly entered, and with the yellowing, trembling fingers of a hand on which the hard, calciferous veins stood out blue and swollen, he'd point to the appropriate columns and figures, indicating to his family that all was in order.

Now, pacing along the asphalt, he no longer carried the white striped woollen blanket or water flask he had prepared for his daughter's journey. Yet he seemed to shoulder a far greater burden. His wife walked frailly beside him as if seeking refuge in the shadow of the walls.

School children scurried through the streets, returning from the First of September Book Fair. They had been to exchange their old school books for new ones and were now chattering and laughing about their teachers, especially the two strictest, Mályvády, the maths and physics master, and Szunyogh, the old drunkard. Classes had not yet begun. Today was the first day of term.

It took the elderly couple the best part of half an hour to trudge back to Petőfi Street where the asphalt came to an end and open ditches, overrun with weeds, gaped on either side of the road. Mihály Veres, their stalwart neighbour, sat out in the street, awl and paring knife in his hands. Veres was a cobbler, a struggling grey-haired craftsman who toiled slowly and moodily from dawn till dusk in his dank subterranean workshop, reached by three brick steps down from the pavement. The musty smell of size wafted out into the street and would even infiltrate the Vajkays' house. The cobbler's horde of rowdy children ran riot in the broad and dirty yard between the pigsties and the empty sheds.

The Vajkay house stood opposite.

This spruce, whitewashed building now slumbered in silence. The five front windows stood shut, the cream lace of the drawn curtains draped over the window cushions which, even in the heat of summer, were never removed.

Ákos rummaged in his pocket for the string of keys he always carried with him and opened the black lattice gate. They passed inside.

He closed the living-room door behind him and carefully replaced the thick wall hanging that was draped, winter and summer, to keep out the draught, from two brass nails on the back of the door.

A hollow interior received them. It was only then they spoke.

'How will we bear it?' said the woman in the narrow hallway, tears already welling in her eyes.

'We'll manage,' Father replied.

'Friday, Saturday, Sunday,' the woman mumbled, as if telling her beads, 'then Monday, Tuesday, Wednesday, Thursday – ' here she paused to sigh – 'then Friday. A week. A whole week, Father. Whatever will we do without her?'

Ákos made no reply. He never spoke much, but felt and thought all the more.

As the woman went on crying, however, he felt obliged to break his silence.

'Come on now, let's not cry. Today's Friday. Friday's tears are Sunday's laughter. And we'll laugh too, Mother, just you see,' he said without a trace of conviction, and disappeared into the dining room.

There stood the table in the bright afternoon sunlight, still covered with the greasy plates, glasses and crumbs left over from lunch. At any other time Skylark would have smartly swept the crumbs away with her little dustpan and brush. But even now, how considerate she had been. Before leaving she had straightened the chairs in the drawing room, made the beds, placed two glasses of water on her parents' bedside table and set nightlight and matches on the old cabinet beside the gold carriage clock for them to light when it got dark.

Mother began tidying her daughter's bedroom. Ákos, unable to settle, gazed vacantly in through the door.

The room had once looked like a chapel, chaste and white.

But the paintwork had faded with time and the silk cushions had grown soiled and a little grey. In the cupboard stood empty cosmetic jars, prayer books from which the lace trimmings of devotional pictures protruded with German inscriptions, velvet-bound, ornamental keepsake albums, fans scribbled thick with names, ball programmes, perfume sachets and hairpieces hanging from a length of string.

Beside the door in the darkest corner of the room, facing north, hung Skylark's mirror.

Everything was engulfed in silence.

'How empty it all seems,' sighed Mother, gesturing with an open hand.

Ákos did not know what to say. As if, over the long years of their marriage, he had lost the power to initiate conversation, he simply repeated:

'How empty.'

They went back into the dining room.

There on the sideboard sparkled their treasures –

'Souvenirs of Lake Velence', 'Souvenirs of Lake Balaton', 'Glasses from Karlsbad' – accumulated over many years and preserved with unconscious piety. All kinds of other odds and ends glittered alongside them, worthless merchandise now utterly useless and inappropriate: fancy bazaar jugs, tiny china dogs, silver-plated goblets, gold-plated angels, all the ghastly icons of provincial life, dusted every day and assembled on small shelves in rows above the back of the sofa. They trembled when anyone sat down, and toppled on to the chest of anyone who unsuspectingly lay down on the sofa beneath them. And then the pictures; how painfully they too stared back at the old couple now. Dobozy, the Hungarian hero, fleeing from the Turks, clasping his wife around her naked breast; the first Hungarian cabinet; and the baldheaded Batthyány, down on his knees with his arms flung wide, waiting for the murderous bullet of his Austrian executioners.

'Let's go into the garden,' the woman proposed.

'Yes, the garden,' echoed Ákos.

They went into the garden. Sweltering, yellow heat greeted them outside. Delicate white kittens pranced across the emerald lawn. A large bowl of water stood beside the well, the sunlight making the colours of the rainbow through the glasses inside. A sunflower on a crooked stem lifted its sun-worshipping head to the blazing west. Horse-chestnut trees, acacias and sumachs rose up behind. And still farther back, by the garden wall, a Virginia pokeweed showed off its dark, ripe berries.

On Skylark's crochet bench they sat down side by side.

'Poor thing,' said Mother, 'at least it'll be a rest. And perhaps . . .' She did not continue.

'Perhaps what?'

'Perhaps someone might . . . turn up.'

'What kind of someone?'

'Someone,' Mother repeated timidly, 'some . . . good fortune,' she added with an affecting, womanly boldness.

Father looked away in irritation, ashamed to hear what he had so often heard in vain, had so often thought himself, yet knew would only ever lead to more humiliating fiascos and bitter disappointments. There was something vulgar about his wife's remark. He shrugged. Then, almost inaudibly, he muttered:

'Absurd.'

He reached for his pocket watch.

'What time did he say?' he asked.

'Who?'

'Him,' the old man barked, and his wife immediately knew he was referring to Géza Cifra.

'Five twenty.'

'It's half past five,' said Father. 'She'll have just got in.'

The thought consoled them both a little. They rose from the bench and strolled among the lilac bushes where a stone dwarf stood on guard. At about this time they usually set off on their walks with Skylark, through the empty streets to the calvary cross and back. But not today. They walked around the garden several times, side by side, their pace quickening as they went. Ákos hoped the horses hadn't bolted on the plain and that Tiger hadn't bitten the girl. Mother ambled along beside him, sharing, and thus lightening, the burden of his thoughts. It felt as if that awful week – a week they'd have to spend alone – had already begun badly, very badly indeed. It all seemed so endless, hopeless and bleak.

Skylark had promised to wire home the moment she arrived. They had written out the message in advance, so all she had to do was send it off. All it said was:

'Arrived safely.'

Dusk fell slowly. For a while they waited for the postman out in the garden, but unable to settle they went inside, believing this would somehow speed the telegram's arrival.

Hours went by and still it hadn't come.

Ákos shut all the doors. As every evening, he checked behind the furniture and the clothes in the wardrobes to see if anyone was hiding there. At nine, when he would usually retire, he went into the bedroom with his wife and lay down on the bed, still fully dressed.

Thoroughly worn out, he fell asleep.

In his dreams he was again walking down Széchenyi Street with Skylark and his wife.

But now they deviated from their usual route and turned into a less familiar road, taking them under a tunnel and, through seemingly endless back streets, into a kind of timber yard.

Here he suddenly noticed that his daughter was

missing. He looked at his wife, whose face at once confirmed his terrible premonitions. The woman's face did not merely suggest the girl had disappeared, but that she had been kidnapped. He had already seen her kidnappers several times, mysterious characters dressed partly like medieval knights in armour and partly like clowns in black face masks.

Ákos started to run ahead towards the timber yard, then, suddenly alarmed to find himself alone, ran back again. For a moment he thought he had seen her. Beside a wooden fence that reminded him of his own, Skylark, like a quiet madwoman, lifted her slanted, imploring gaze towards him and, reaching out with her hands, cried for help. She appeared to be trapped. Ákos was just about to reach out to her when she disappeared.

After that he searched for her in vain. He rattled gates, inquired at inns, even entered one suspicious-looking house, a kind of suburban brothel, where ugly strumpets cackled at him before turning on him with their fists. Finally he found himself in a strange work-shop at the bottom of a flight of steps, deep beneath the ground.

Here in a green apron squatted an artisan, not Mr Veres, but a sly and shifty individual in a regulation cap with a tin number. He clearly knew all there was to know, and, without even looking at Ákos, pointed with conspiratorial indifference to a curtained glass door. Ákos charged through it and, in a dim alcove, finally found his daughter. Skylark lay on the ground, her head shaven, her body horribly mutilated, stab wounds in her naked breast. She was dead.

The old woman quietly pottered about the room, careful not to wake her husband. She could hear his irregular breathing – the sort that often heralds a sleeping cry – and watched his restless head turn on the pillow. Her husband's first sleep tended to be nightmarish, and he'd often spring up in bed with an animal howl.

She went over to him, bent down and lightly touched his brow.

Ákos sat up. He took a sip of water.

He kept his eyes wide open.

He could still see before him the figures from his dream, whom he had encountered so many times before. But even now it staggered him that his precious daughter, who, poor thing, lived such a quiet life, could be the focus of such a horrific and dramatic dream.

After these nightmares he would love Skylark still more dearly.

His wife spoke of the telegram.

'Still nothing?' asked Ákos.

'Not yet.'

At this the bell buzzed in the kitchen. The woman sprang up and ran to open the door.

'It's here,' she cried, hurrying back.

'Arrived safely.'

She read it aloud.

Ákos took it into his hands and gazed at it with happy, unbelieving eyes.

'*Arrived safely.*'

He, too, read it out loud.

Fully reassured and smiling at their earlier fears, they undressed, put out the light and both dozed off to sleep.

And high time too; it was already after midnight.

IV

in which some of the more notable figures of Sárszeg
appear before us in the King of Hungary, one Bálint
Környey among them

O n Saturday the town was flooded with people
from the surrounding farms. Saturday was
market day.

It was still dark when the first women arrived. Rattling down the unpaved streets in their carts, they
dragged a train of dust behind them. First they fed
their brood of bawling infants who bounced among
the kohlrabi in the depths of their wicker-ribbed
wagons. Pulling flat milk bottles from their boots, the
teats already swarming black with flies, they pressed
them into the tiny mouths of their hungry offspring,
who greedily gulped down the warm, sour milk.

Some time later the peasants from Kék strolled in.
They congregated around the gossips' bench on Széchenyi Square and, with squat clay pipes jutting from
their fanglike teeth, they rambled on about rinderpest
and rising taxes. Beside them, in a separate group,

stood the local artisans and tradesmen, complaining about the shortage of cash, which couldn't be raised anywhere these days, because their lordships were playing it safe and kept their money in the Agricultural Bank at 5 per cent interest.

The market seethed in the sweltering heat, humming with noise and ablaze with every imaginable colour. Red peppers shone as brightly as the florid scarlet paint in the paint-shop window across the square. Cabbages displayed their pale-green, silken frills, violet grapes glistened, marrows whitened in the sun, and yellowing melons, already past their best, gave off a sickly choleroid stench. Farther off, towards Petőfi Street, stood the butchers' stalls where truncated carcasses swung with raw, barbaric pomp from iron hooks, and barrel-chested butchers' boys in skimpy vests shattered bones with heavy mallets. From Bólyai Street, where the potters gathered, came the clatter of the crockery stalls. Everywhere poultry pecked, maids gossiped and gentlewomen moaned about impossible prices. Above them all stretched a veil of silvery grey dust, Sárszeg's murderous dust which robbed so many local children of their lives and brought the adults to an early death.

Miklós Ijas, assistant editor of the *Sárszeg Gazette* at barely twenty-four, viewed this scene through the plate-glass windows of the Széchenyi Café. He wore a modish English suit, a turned-down collar and a slender lilac necktie.

He had woken at half past nine and immediately hurried to the café to read the Budapest papers.

Although he'd had no breakfast, he ordered rum with his black coffee and lit one cigarette after another. His lip curled with disgust.

He saw this same scene every day. The celebrities of Sárszeg swam past his plate-glass window as if in an aquarium.

First came Galló, the prosecutor, on his way to court, bareheaded, with a flat brown briefcase in his hand. With a furrowed brow and an affable smile he was rehearsing a stern indictment speech against some heinous Swabian highwayman. Fashionable townsfolk passed slowly by with ivory-knobbed canes. Priboczay was already standing in the doorway of the St Mary Pharmacy, performing his daily manicure with a penknife. Feri Füzes was hurrying towards the Gentlemen's Club.

Feri Füzes was to meet the opponent's seconds in the club dining room so that statements could be drawn up and the thorny affair, which had been dragging on for weeks, could finally be settled, for better or worse, according to the proper protocol. Provocation, duel, court of honour, sabres, plastrons, five paces forward, to the finish – these were the words that buzzed through Feri Füzes's head as his pointed patent-leather shoes creaked their way across the asphalt.

It was he who patched up Sárszeg's wounded prides and damaged honours; the perfect gentleman, a regular cavalier. He exuded eau de cologne and cavorted about with a foolish, sickly grin that never left his lips. He wore his smile just as he wore his chic boater in summer or his fancy spats in winter.

County carriages flew by. Liverymen sat up on the boxes in dapper blue and white-piped uniforms, their hat ribbons fluttering in the wind. Then the burly figure of a gentleman with a bushy, yellow moustache appeared on the pavement of Széchenyi Street. Bálint Környey.

By profession, Bálint Környey was commander in chief of the local fire brigade. But in reality he occupied a far more elevated position in Sárszeg society. He was everybody's friend or acquaintance and turned up absolutely everywhere. President of the Panthers' Table, fabled drinker, fêted sportsman, he could break a silver forint coin in two with his bare hands. It was he who set the prizes for the Sárszeg Student Games, and he who organised the Grand Venetian Night with floodlights and fireworks on Tarliget Lake each summer. Even now the billboards were still plastered with tattered flyers announcing this splendid July event to the citizens of Sárszeg.

He greeted the young editor with a wave of his stick. Ijas returned the greeting coolly. To local people he was just an editor; they had no idea what a poet he was.

The clocks had struck eleven in Petőfi Street and still all was silent. Even Mr Veres sensed this silence from the depths of his dark, insalubrious workshop. The Vajkays usually rose on the dot of seven. Skylark would open all the windows, airing and cleaning the rooms inside.

Today the old couple had overslept. The nightlight still flickered beside the carriage clock.

When they first opened their eyes it was already twenty to twelve. They were surprised to find themselves alone. For a moment they pricked up their ears, but no sound came from their daughter's room next door. The anxieties of the previous day still hung heavy on their hearts, and as they woke they lived the whole day over again.

But another, no less painful sensation now presented itself besides. Their stomachs began to rumble: a loud, hollow sound, silencing all other complaints and demanding their undivided attention.

While they slept, dreams had provided illusory nourishment, smothering their hunger with thick and coloured veils. But no sooner had they dressed than they could feel their emptiness, and pressed their palms against their burning stomachs.

'I'm starving,' said father.

'Me too,' said Mother.

And they laughed at their own frailty.

No wonder they were famished. They had forgotten supper the evening before and had only pecked hurriedly at lunch. Such meals are never filling.

'Quickly, tea.'

'Yes, tea.'

Mother went into the kitchen to make tea.

The Vajkays didn't keep a maid. Skylark's nanny, Örzse, a liveryman's daughter, who had been with them since the age of twenty, had left them six years before. Since then they had taken on the odd girl here and there, but these never stayed more than a couple of weeks. Skylark was so strict, keeping everything locked away, especially the sugar, and so demanding that the maids all fled before their time was up. They didn't want a new girl in their home now; after all, they had to be careful with money, had to count every penny. Besides, the girls all stole and gossiped nowadays. And anyway, what could a maid do that they could not? Skylark and her mother did everything themselves, and better too. Cleaning was a joy, and as for cooking, they loved nothing more. They were always boiling or baking something.

Mother and Father drank their tea. But this did not stave off their hunger. It merely cleansed their stomachs, increasing the emptiness. Their thoughts turned at once to lunch.

Already some weeks earlier it had been agreed that, for these few days – it was only a week, after all – they wouldn't cook at home. Skylark, who presided in all culinary matters, recommended the King of Hungary, Sárszeg's largest restaurant, as the one place where the cuisine was still tolerable.

The three of them detested restaurants. And although they had hardly visited this one, they could talk about it for hours with sneering condescension. The dishwater soups, the tough and gristly meat, the carelessly concocted desserts they served up to poor, unsuspecting bachelors, who had never tasted *good home cooking*. Not to mention the disgusting state of the kitchens. Oh, for a home-made soup, a home-made stew, or a home-baked pastry! They had often expressed such sentiments to Géza Cifra.

Somehow they had to overcome the disgust they

had artificially cultivated beyond all proportion. On the way to the restaurant they comforted each other, braving themselves for the dubious event. When they stepped inside the King of Hungary they immediately wrinkled their noses and screwed up their eyes. An enormous, clean and friendly dining hall stretched out before them, with a ceiling of frosted glass, lit, even by day, by four weighty chandeliers.

Ákos led his wife to a table and sat down.

In the middle of the impeccably laundered tablecloth stood a bunch of flowers. Beside it were two small silver dishes freshly heaped with salt and paprika, a pepper pot and jars of mustard, vinegar and oil. To one side, on a splendid glass platter with a silver rim, lay apples, peaches and, in little wicker baskets, fresh and crusty rolls, salted croissants and small white loaves sprinkled with poppy seeds. Just then two pastry boys came through the door in bright white caps, carrying a long wooden board packed with a battalion of vanilla slices, whose rich egg fillings shone a gorgeous gold beneath their crumbling red-brown pastry crusts, sprinkled thick with icing sugar. The old man stole a fleeting glance at these delights with a certain vague contempt. He picked up the menu, then handed it to his wife.

'You order. I can't even bring myself to look.'

'What would you like?'

'Whatever,' Ákos mumbled, 'Whatever you want. It makes no difference to me.'

He looked around him. It wasn't an entirely

43

unpleasant place. Certainly not as bad as he had imagined.

By now nearly all the tables were full. He recognised no one, and no one recognised him. They lived in such seclusion that they almost counted as strangers. And they felt like strangers too; as if they had stumbled into the restaurant of some altogether unfamiliar town.

Then Ákos did spot one acquaintance. Opposite, all on his own, sat Weisz and Partner. Old Mr Weisz went everywhere alone, without his partner, whom few had ever seen. But everyone called him Weisz and Partner all the same.

Looking up from the cloud of tepid steam that rose from the silver bowl before him and misted up his pince-nez, Weisz and Partner greeted Ákos with an absent-minded nod of the head. He was utterly engrossed in the serious business of eating. He stared wide-eyed at the neatly diced red meat of his goulash soup as he ladled it into a porcelain bowl printed with the curlicued monogram KH. Using the back of his soup spoon, he mashed his perfect egg-shaped potatoes into a smooth puree. He ate quickly and with great relish. The remaining, wonderfully oily liquid he mopped up with morsels of bread roll pinned to his fork.

The waiter arrived at the Vajkays' table and poured a clear consommé into their plates. Small pea-shaped croutons, made of pancake mix tossed in fat, swam on its glistening surface. They ordered chicken risotto, which they often made at home, followed by bread-

and-butter pudding. Ákos ate with a healthy appetite and was not slow to clean his plate.

'How was it?' asked his wife, who felt herself unqualified to judge in such matters. She was the lightest of eaters, and would only nibble from the tip of her fork.

'Passable,' the old man replied. 'Actually quite . . .' For a moment his voice became higher, more enthusiastic, then he seemed to change his mind. 'Quite passable,' he concluded, correcting himself in time.

After paying the bill, they sat at their table for a while looking sombre and a little bemused.

The silvery clattering of cutlery resounded all around. The diners dug into their meals with great conviction, aware that they were carrying out a most important task. Lonely men sat jealously guarding their dishes; whole families made themselves thoroughly at home, tying napkins around the necks of their little boys and girls.

Ákos repeatedly leaned over to his wife:

'Who's that?'

'Don't know.'

'And him?'

'Don't know him either.'

Beside them sat a group of army officers, recently returned from the garrison at Bilek.

The dashing young men munched crusty rolls between their strong white teeth and lifted anchovies with their toothpicks from the oily depths of narrow tins. Ákos observed them gloomily. As soon as they began to laugh, he lowered his gaze. Their glances

offended him. They belonged to a world of happy
households, eligible daughters and handsome dowries;
a world so very different from his own. To disguise
the discomfort he felt whenever they turned his way,
he picked up the menu and read it wearily from top to
bottom.

In a far corner of the restaurant, beside a potted palm
tree and beneath a portrait of Franz Josef dressed in
Hungarian military garb, sat a larger gathering, who
lunched here every day at noon. The waiters swarmed
around them, bowing and scraping eagerly. Chewing
at spicy sausages and knuckles of pork, they knocked
back one mug of beer after another. Here Ákos recognised two more acquaintances. One was their family
physician, Dr Gál, a short-sighted man who divided
his time, in the most fashionable of circles, between
the café, the restaurant and the theatre. Exactly when
he found time to see his patients remained a mystery.
The other was Priboczay, the quiet, convivial pharmacist, who took his place at table as the Panthers' deputy
president. He sat passively nodding his head, whose
thinning fair hair had lost its lustre years before but still
refused to go grey and shone a pale lilac colour as if it
were dyed.

But the cream of Sárszeg society were also present.

Papa Fehér, manager of the local branch of the Agricultural Bank; Prosecutor Galló, who had already
delivered his stern indictment speech against the heinous Swabian highwayman; and many others.

Feri Füzes had settled the conditions for the duel,
and very grave they were, too. Gentleman that he was,

he spoke of this to no one – apart from Dr Gál, whom he drew to one side at the corner of the long table, where, grinning more broadly than ever, he announced that two gentlemen would be crossing swords at dawn, at the accustomed spot in Sárszeg forest, and that the good doctor might care to stand by with his surgical instruments at the ready. To the finish, naturally, to the finish.

The door swung open every five minutes, and the new arrival would disappear into this billowing gathering of men.

Just after one o'clock, when school had finished, the teachers began to arrive: Mályvády, the maths and physics master, and Szunyogh, the Latin teacher.

Dr Gál instructed the latter to sit down beside him at once. Without uttering a word he clasped Szunyogh's wrist between his forefinger and thumb, and, holding his gold pocket watch in his left hand, began earnestly taking the teacher's pulse.

Poor Szunyogh was already in a wretched state. Some two years earlier he had begun to exhibit the unmistakable symptoms of delirium tremens, and his family had carted him off to a sanatorium. There he made a slight recovery, but as soon as he was out again he slumped back into his old illness.

There was a time when he had shown prodigious talent, but in Sárszeg he had surrendered himself to the bottle and become a notorious alcoholic. His students whispered that he kept a hip flask in his pocket and would dash out into the corridor during lessons to take a swig or two. For months now he had been unable to sleep; he could never get warm and, even throughout the summer, wore a thick overcoat and lined his shoes with cotton wool so his feet wouldn't freeze. His puffy cheeks and double chin glowed brick red, and his baby-blue eyes swam with tears. He was always drunk well before noon.

His ice-cold wrist trembled in the doctor's warm hand. He sat there in the restaurant, the collar of his winter coat turned up, gazing as sheepishly at the doctor as his students gazed at him.

Dr Gál pressed the lid of his pocket watch shut with a quiet, golden click. He looked Szunyogh in the eye. As always he appealed to the teacher's better self. One by one he extolled the beauties of life, reminding Szunyogh of his wife and charming daughter. He spoke of the teacher's former ambition, of the articles he had once published in the *Philological Review*. And he did nothing to disguise the horrid fate that would soon await his friend if he failed to change his ways. Szunyogh listened attentively, his blond eyelashes blinking, his torso swaying to and fro, and his emaciated legs shivering beneath the table. Accepting the physician's sound advice, he ordered himself a modest glass of table wine.

The Vajkays were just about to leave when Bálint Környey strode in, accompanied by two other gentlemen.

One was Szolyvay, the popular comedian. The other was a tall and smartly dressed actor in an elegant top hat. He was Imre Zányi, the celebrated leading man, the idol of every woman and girl in Sárszeg.

Until then the gathering had been growing increasingly spirited; but now the general din soared to new heights. Környey was greeted with a thundering roar of laughter, properly befitting the arrival of the Table's honoured president. For his part, Környey stood before his companions, hands behind his back, as if inspecting his Panther troops.

'Greetings, gentlemen.'

The Panthers' Table had been formed some twenty years before, with the not unworthy aim of popularising the consumption of alcohol and promoting gentlemanly friendship.

The Panthers were expected to drink daily and diligently, whether they could hold their drink or not. Ákos had been a member once himself, at the very beginning, when the Table was first founded. But he had suddenly grown old, 'soured', as the others complained, and no longer paid them any attention. Many more had fallen by the wayside, collapsing from chronic alcohol poisoning and cirrhosis of the liver, which was how most men in Sárszeg met their end. Every year the Table laid wreaths at their graves. During Környey's touching speeches the younger Panther cubs would come close to tears, as did those veterans who, in spite of their snowy hair, still stood their ground and were Panthers to the last.

Bálint Környey sat down among them. He had a friendly word for everyone. Then suddenly, as he was about to raise his tankard to his lips, he spotted Ákos, the dear old friend and companion of his youth. He broke into a smile, then fell back into his seat. Of all the . . . He gave Ákos a hearty wave and then, in good country fashion, bellowed over to his table:

'Greetings! Greetings, old chap!'

They no longer had much to do with each other these days. At most, Környey would send Ákos a brace of pheasant or partridge when he had been out hunting on his estate.

But they were both clearly pleased to see each other now.

At Környey's greeting the Panthers quietened down a little. They leaned towards their beloved president, who was explaining something to his neighbours, clearly about the character he had just greeted. The Panthers glanced respectfully, if perhaps a little sadly, at the Vajkays' lonely table. Then Bálint Környey rose to his feet.

'My dear old Ákos! Welcome!' he called out before reaching the table and bending down to kiss the hand of his friend's good lady. Then he shook hands with Ákos himself. 'This is a turn-up for the books,' he said with a chuckle. 'What brings you here?'

'Lunch,' Ákos stuttered. 'We came for lunch.' After this he began to hum and haw.

'You wicked old Panther,' Környey interrupted, shaking a huge finger at Ákos, 'you've been unfaithful to us. Why don't you look in at the Club some time?'

'Forgive me, my friend, but I no longer drink, nor smoke, nor play cards. And what is more –' here Ákos paused momentarily for thought – 'I've grown old.'

The two friends nodded in silence, showing each

other the monkish tonsures that parted their thinning hair.

For a while they reminisced about old times, legendary evenings and long-lost friends. Környey, however, was soon called back to his table. He humbly begged their pardon. The Vajkays had anyway been about to leave.

They wandered out into the street.

Somewhere in the north it had been raining and the oppressive heat had abated. Everything was flooded in a soft and pleasant light. Ákos straightened his back and breathed the air deep into his lungs. A sudden warmth spread through his limbs as his digestive system set to work. The food he had eaten was already filtering its fortifying goodness into his circulation.

The interest that had met the couple in the restaurant followed them out into the street. Strangers turned to look at them as they passed. Not that there was anything unusual about their appearance. People simply weren't accustomed to seeing them there in the street, like old couches that belong in the living room and look so strange when, once or twice a year, they're put outside to air.

They didn't hurry. They strolled sedately on the swept asphalt, criss-crossed with clinker bricks, returning the greetings of afternoon strollers who seemed to have become more amicable with the passing of the dreadful heat. They gave themselves up to the easy afternoon atmosphere.

The bells were ringing. Ding-dong, the bells rang constantly in Sárszeg. At morning Mass, at vespers, at funerals . . . so many funerals. There were three coffin-makers in Széchenyi Street, one after the other, and two stonemason's yards. Hearing the endless peal of deafening bells and seeing all these funeral concerns, the unsuspecting visitor might have imagined that people didn't live in Sárszeg at all, but only died there. Meanwhile the dealers sat inside their shops, among the coffins and tombstones, with the blind faith, shared by all in their profession, that it was precisely their wares everybody needed. And secure in this blithe conviction, they made their handsome fortunes, brought up their broods of children and kept their families in considerable style. Ákos peered through the open door of one such concern. Bronze coffins catering for every shape and size, from the tallest adult to the smallest child, stood upended in a tidy row. The shopkeeper was smoking a cigar, his wife reading a newspaper, while their angora cat sat preening itself inside an open wooden coffin. It wasn't such a terrible sight.

A slanting shaft of sunlight tumbled through the thick glass jars of the St Mary Pharmacy. On the painted signboard outside, the name of Priboczay shone in thick gold letters. Beneath it stood an image of Mary, the pharmacy's patron saint, trampling a snake underfoot, with the pagan Aesculapius close by. Everything glistened.

Every imaginable monstrosity. Even the display of surgical instruments sparkled: glittering silver forceps, shiny rubber gloves, gleaming collapsible operating tables. An anatomical dummy, with twinkling amethyst glass eyes in its trephined skull, proudly displayed its bloody heart, its bistre liver and green gall bladder, and the twisting intestines of its lacerated stomach. The Vajkays had never dared look at all this before. But now they did look. And it was horrible. Horrible, yet interesting.

Then the other window displays – how enticing they all seemed! So many messages and promises beaming out towards them. What can I do for you, sir; at your service, madam; all life's paraphernalia, take your pick. Brand-new goods, never been touched, to replace the old and worn. Silk purses, exquisite velvets and first-class fabrics in tasteful piles, handkerchiefs and walking sticks, perfume bottles tied with satin ribbon bows, meerschaum pipes and humidors, scrunchy cigars and gold-tipped cigarettes.

They stopped in front of Weisz and Partner's, admiring a pigskin suitcase with an English press-stud lock, so different from the shabby old canvas cases they had at home. And then that crocodile-skin handbag. The woman simply couldn't tear herself away. How splendid, how absolutely charming! Ákos drew his wife gently by the arm; it was time to move on.

Among the notepads and pencil cases in the window of Mr Vajna's stationery store stood rows of books whose covers had already faded in the blistering sun. These literary novelties from Budapest came as quite a shock to the old man, who had long grown used to the arid, antiquated style of his noble records, deeds and documents. Fierce and fashionable volumes of poetry glared back at him with diabolical, sneering faces;

naked male bodies and delirious women with their hair down and their staring eyes wide open.

Ákos read their phoney, pseudo-modern titles over and over again: *Deathrun – In the Night of Life, Aspasia Mine: I Want You!* The woman nudged her husband with a smile. But Ákos only shrugged. Yes, such things existed. He found them strange, but couldn't conceal a certain curiosity.

At home they put on their slippers, caught their breath and rested. So much had happened in one day.

The sun was still shining. They opened a window and a tepid current of air streamed through the house, leaving columns of golden dust in its wake. One of Veres's ragged, grimy brats loafed around in the yard outside. He was gnawing at a slice of dry bread, down which the thick sunlight trickled like honey. The boy seemed to be catching the drips with his tongue. In the distance, the sound of a Gypsy band.

The two of them listened together.

'Music,' said Mother.

'Yes,' Father replied. 'Someone's living it up.'

'Hear it? "If I had a little farm . . ." '

When it began to grow dark, Ákos fetched the Budapest newspaper from the letterbox.

They took only one paper; Ákos's father had ordered it long ago, and it had become a kind of family tradition ever since. In those days it still stood for the values and interests of the Hungarian nobility. But much water had run under the bridge since then, and the paper had switched direction several times. It was hardly recognisable now, and preached the opposite of its original convictions. This fact, however, had escaped the old man's attention.

He spoke of the paper with inveterate deference, and when he opened the wrapper with his penknife an expression of pious rapture spread across his face. He reverently immersed himself in the odd article, and if by chance he found his social class disparaged, he convinced himself he hadn't fully understood, and went on nodding as he read, blithely turning the pages, reluctant to dissent. In truth, he had grown a little indifferent to the news. He no longer read the paper from cover to cover, only skimmed over the headlines to the marriage and death columns at the back. After a while he wearied of this too, and wouldn't touch the paper for weeks on end. Countless issues lay strewn over the table, unopened.

Today, however, he had risen late and, in spite of all his comings and goings, was still not tired. He slowly browsed his way through the entire paper.

However, he couldn't see too well. The Vajkays' chandelier hung close to the ceiling, high above the dining-room table. They had taken out three of the four light bulbs to save on electricity. In other matters the couple were less frugal, but on this one saving they rigorously insisted. And so they groped around in perpetual semi-darkness.

'I can't see,' Ákos complained.

'Perhaps you should put in the other bulbs.'

Ákos climbed up on the table and steadied the chandelier. Suddenly all four bulbs were shining brightly. A warm even light flooded the dining room.

'How cosy,' the woman cried.

'Indeed,' replied Father. 'Now we can read.'

The old man put on his spectacles and began to read aloud to his wife.

The Dreyfus affair. Second hearing before the military tribunal at Rennes. That notorious French captain. Handed secret documents over to the Germans. Accused of high treason. To answer for his crimes before the court. Talk of the death sentence.

The woman wasn't interested.

'Kaiser Wilhelm in Alsace-Lorraine.'

'The German Kaiser?'

'The very same. Says the territory always was and always would be German.'

'Alsace-Lorraine?'

'Alsace-Lorraine, Mother, which they took back from the French in 1871. Goodness, we were young then. I was forty.'

Ákos smiled. The woman smiled too. She rested her palm lightly on the old man's hand.

'There won't be another war, will there?' The woman sighed.

'The French and the Germans,' Ákos explained, 'have never cared much for each other. But they seem to have settled their differences this time.'

Foreign news items flashed up before them, charging the air they breathed with a buzz of electricity, connecting the couple to the burning, bitter, but not entirely ignominious or worthless, affairs of the outside world. They didn't understand much of what they read, but felt none the less that they were not entirely

alone. Millions struggled just like them. And it was
here that all those struggles found a common meeting
place.

'Strike,' said Ákos. 'An English word. Pronounced
strahyk. The workers don't want to work.'

'Why not?'

'Because they don't want to.'

'Why don't they make them?'

Ákos shrugged.

'Goodness, Mother,' he said in a low voice, adjust-
ing his spectacles on the bridge of his nose, 'five thousand workers are on strike in Brazil. "The employers
have adamantly refused to meet their demands." '

'Poor things,' said Mother, not really knowing
whom she pitied, the workers or the employers.

Anyway, as the papers reported every month, they
had discovered a new and infallible cure for tubercu-
losis. Which only went to show there was progress
after all.

'Phew,' Ákos sighed. 'Here, too. "Shameless agitators among our people." "Peasants promised half an
acre in the name of the prime minister." They're calling it "communism". They want to redistribute the
land.'

'Who do?'

Enough of politics. They were more interested in
tragedies and disasters.

' "In the state of Ohio," ' Father read, ' "a train
plunged from a railway bridge. Two dead and thirty
severely injured." '

'Dreadful,' said Mother, who gave a sudden shudder and came close to tears.

'And how *are* all those poor injured people?' she asked.

They both took a closer look at the paper, but found nothing.

'Doesn't say,' Father mumbled.

At all events, they came alive in this flood of common human hopes and fears. It revived them, dispersing the stifling dullness that had eaten into their bodies, their clothes and all their furniture.

They both stared into space.

'How are you feeling, Mother?' asked Ákos.

'I'm coping, Father,' the woman replied. 'And you?'

'Me too.'

Ákos went over to his wife and softly kissed her forehead.

When it was time to light the nightlight they couldn't find the matches. They always kept them on the old cabinet, beside the carriage clock. But now they weren't in their proper place. The woman searched every nook and cranny. At last she found them in the kitchen. She had taken them with her in the morning to make tea, and had forgotten to return them to the cabinet. She hurried back to the bedroom and handed the matches to her husband.

Then they looked at each other as if something had suddenly occurred to them

But they didn't say a word.

V

---

*in which Ákos Vajkay of Kisvajka and Köröshegy
eats goulash soup, breast of veal and vanilla noodles,
and lights a cigar*

Sárszeg is a tiny dot on the map. Apart from a
small conservatoire and a third-rate public
library, it boasts of no curiosities at all. Most
people have either never heard of it, or mention it with
disdain. But every Sunday morning, in the clear blue
sky before the church of St Stephen, the good Lord
hovers above the town, invisible and merciful,
righteous and terrible, ever present and everywhere
the same, be it in Sárszeg or in Budapest, in Paris or
New York.

Low Mass begins at half past eleven.

It is attended by the upper crust of Sárszeg society:
county dignitaries, senior civil servants and other well-
to-do citizens who have distinguished themselves from
their fellow mortals. They are accompanied by their
wives and nubile daughters, who in turn are followed
by spruce young men, secret suitors who converge

behind the pillars in the background and gather around the font. The girls sit beside their mothers, casting the occasional glance at their prayer books, leaning back in their seats, eyes to heaven, sighing at every sounding of the carillon. They dab their eyes with tiny handkerchiefs as if in tears. Pungent perfumes bolt through the air, one answering the other. A veritable concert of fragrances. Which is why they often called it 'scented Mass'. It wasn't merely a matter of spiritual elevation; it was a social event.

The Vajkays' absence from church did not pass unnoticed. Their customary place, at the end of the second bench on the right, remained unoccupied.

In his damp, courtyard-facing study, Ákos lay on the Turkish rug which covered his couch. It was an uncomfortable couch, short and narrow, like all their furniture. It couldn't even accommodate Ákos's spindly frame. The only way he could stretch out his legs was to hoist them over the back rest. But Ákos had grown so used to this position he hardly noticed it any more.

Although he wasn't cold, he wrapped himself in a thick camel-hair blanket. He gazed up at the patterns on the ceiling, then, wearying of this, reached out, without rising, towards his bookshelf, and from among his numerous volumes of *Aristocratic Families* and the *Almanach de Gotha*, pulled out Volume XIV, by Iván Nagy, on the families of Hungary. He thumbed through it listlessly.

The book provided no surprises. He already knew

its every detail, every letter, inside out. The volume soon fell from his hands, and Ákos began to ruminate:

'Vanilla noodles. What exactly can they be? I've never tried them, never even seen them. I've no idea how they might taste. Vanilla I'm fond of. That strange, almost exciting smell. Must be rather nice to have the smell tickle the nose while the taste flatters the tongue. I wonder if they serve the yellowish noodles with that black African spice sprinkled on top? I've only ever glimpsed the name, in passing, between the curd dumplings, fruit sorbets and hazelnut gateaux. As if I'd dreamed it somewhere. Still can't get it out of my mind.'

He knitted his brow and tried to banish these silly, demeaning thoughts from his mind.

'Skylark's a good cook. That's undeniable. At least, everyone says so. Of course she is. And not just good, first-rate. They can't find words enough to praise her cooking. In the old days, when we still invited folk for dinner, they made quite a song and dance about it. Even that scoundrel Géza Cifra. Yes, even him. It's true her methods are . . . unusual. She never uses paprika, for example, or pepper, or any other spices. And she's rather sparing with fat as well. She's economical, that's all. And quite right, too. Our modest savings won't last for ever and she can't, mustn't, touch her dowry. I simply wouldn't let her. Certainly not. Besides, heavy food is bad for you. Nice light French cuisine, that's what we like.'

He sat up and sniffed the air around him. Strange. The smells of the restaurant still lingered about his nose, stubbornly, unavoidably, assertively. That stuffy fragrance, fragrant stuffiness, that cruel, aromatic combination of caraway, onions fried in fat, and the pleasantly bitter hop breath of beer. He leaned back on his pillow.

'*Noix de veau.* Another puzzle. One imagines walnut segments, sweet and oily, but that's not what it is. Soft, juicy pieces of tender meat that melt at once in the mouth. Not to be sneezed at. Especially after one of those tempting hors d'oeuvres on the menu. Crayfish bisque, caviar à la russe. Absurd, macabre names. Scrambled eggs with chicken livers, pike in white wine, brains in browned butter. Enough. Enough of this stuff and nonsense.'

He straightened his pillow and sought a more comfortable position.

'Skylark has a weak stomach, poor thing. Although she's plump, she can't take heavy food. And she's often sick. It's in all our interests to eat sensibly. And just think of her wonderfully nourishing fricassees and risottos. Especially the risottos. Ah, the risottos. And her pale sponge fingers. And semolina puddings. No one could say she starved us. Not in the least. If only they served food like that in restaurants. Actually, it wasn't *so* bad there . . . but at home. Yes, good home cooking.'

Ákos had grown tired. He shut his eyes and surrendered himself to whatever came to mind.

'Yesterday, for example. What did we have yesterday? Consommé, chicken risotto, bread-and-butter pudding. I remember exactly. Nothing more, nothing better. Now Weisz and Partner, he had something else. Goulash, that's what it was. Delicious, to be sure: rich, blood-red goulash soup with hot paprika from Szeged, the liquid dripping from his steaming potatoes. How I adored that in my younger days, when poor Mama was still alive. Goulash soup, veal and beef stew – God only knows when I had them last. I never dared ask for things like that. Out of consideration for *her*, I suppose. Not even when we went to a restaurant.'

His eyes welled with tears as if something had stirred inside him.

'Is it a sin? They say the devil torments the fasting hermit. If it is a sin, it's all the sweeter for being so. What do I care? One can't deny these things exist. Goulash soup exists, out there in the world, on the table, on Weisz and Partner's plate. And on the menu too, between the saddles of mutton and herdsmen's cutlets. Beside the tenderloins of pork and the rump steaks. And then all the other things on the menu – they exist too. The sides of pork, the Transylvanian mixed grills, the lamb chops. Not to mention all the dishes with English, French, and Italian names: beefsteaks, tournedos, fritto misto, breathing their foreign aromas. Then the cheeses, light and creamy, thick and heavy, the Camemberts, the Bries, the Port-Saluts; and the wines, red Bull's Blood from Eger, sweet muscatels, light Chardonnays, and Fair Maid from Badacsony, in tall and slender bottles. Fair Maid. Beloved Fair Maid. Ah, my sweet, Fair Maid . . .'

The door opened.

The woman came in from her cleaning. She had been doing the housework all morning. It was now past one and she had only just finished. She was clearly out of practice.

She entered quietly. She thought her husband must have dozed off. But Ákos's eyes opened in alarm at the noise.

'Were you asleep?' asked the woman.

'No.'

'I thought you were asleep.'

'I wasn't.'

'You look pale.'

'Nonsense.'

'Is something the matter?'

Ákos rose from the couch with a guilty conscience, like a child caught up to some prank in bed. He didn't dare meet his wife's gaze, he felt so ashamed.

'You're hungry,' said the woman. 'That's what is is. You're hungry, my dear. You haven't eaten again. Not since last night. Let's go to the restaurant. It's getting late. We won't get a table.'

They hurried. It surprised them how quickly they reached the King of Hungary. They found the restaurant in utter commotion. Plates clattered, wine stewards scurried and waiters scampered. Even the head waiter flitted to and fro on the swallow's wings of his tailcoat. He scribbled calculations on the back of a cigarette box, gave change, plucking silver coins from his palm, listened to complaints and trotted into the kitchens only to re-emerge moments later to reassure his customers that all was well. In spite of the regular

Sunday commotion, his expression remained as calm and collected as ever.

The Vajkays headed towards the table they had taken the day before. But there sat a spirited threesome already well into their meal. That was all they needed. All the other tables were taken too. They waited. But on Sundays, in the comforting knowledge that Sunday is a day of rest, people eat more studiously than at other times. They spend that little bit longer picking their teeth and rolling bread pellets with which they are content to play for hours.

With a few clipped words the head waiter begged their pardon, before taking off again on his swallow's wings.

The woman suggested they might look in on the other restaurant in town, the Baross. Ákos paced sulkily up and down; he was frightfully hungry, and the sight of all the food only fired his appetite. Suddenly two arms began to wave in the air towards him. At the horseshoe table beside the palm trees the enormous figure of Bálint Környey rose to his feet and called out to them:

'Over here!'

'Won't we be intruding?'

'Of course not. Come and sit down; we've already finished. Here, or over there.'

The Panthers had finished lunch and the table was thick with crumbs. Now they only smoked and sipped their drinks. At the Vajkays' arrival they all rose to receive their new guests, even Szunyogh who, owing to his state of perpetual inebriation and his 180 pounds, found it hard to move on his spindly legs. A series of introductions followed.

As hosts the Panthers were most obliging. They rang for the waiters, who immediately swept the table, brought clean plates and glasses, and pressed menus into the hands of the new arrivals.

Ákos sat at one end of the table between the commander in chief and Szolyvay, the comic actor.

Mrs Vajkay sat at the head of the table beside Priboczay, the lilac-haired pharmacist from whom she bought digestive tonics and face powder for Skylark. Her other neighbour was a tall, elegant gentleman in a top hat. She had noticed him the day before, but didn't know who he was. Even now she hadn't caught his name.

The gentleman ceremoniously kissed her hand, as was customary with a lady of repute, and thoroughly overwhelmed her with his refined and unobtrusive attentiveness. He recommended one dish and advised against another; as one who dined there every day, he knew the kitchen intimately.

His face was candid and reassuring. He must have just been shaved, for traces of rice powder could still be seen on his chin and the not unpleasant fragrance of the barber's shop still wafted from his skin.

Suddenly the head waiter came over to him, whispered something in his ear, then drew him aside to one corner of the restaurant. Here the waiter handed him a letter, to which a courier was awaiting a reply. The letter was from Olga Orosz, the prima donna with whom he had been living over the summer. She had to

see him now, just one more time, before they parted
for ever. Would he be so kind as to hurry to her at
once? Her formality of expression was a mark of their
estrangement. Imre Zányi crumpled the letter into his
pocket and signalled that there was no reply. He was
used to farces of this kind.

Mrs Vajkay took advantage of his absence to ask the
pharmacist the young man's name. Hearing that it was
Imre Zányi, the leading man, she was thunderstruck.
She had – as she explained to Priboczay – initially
imagined him to be some youthful priest, but his
fashionable morning coat and unaffected, wordly
manner had immediately led her to suspect otherwise.
So it was he! She had never seen him on stage, but had
heard a great deal about him.

The actor returned to his place at the table. He continued to devote his every attention to the woman,
asking her questions and listening to her replies with
his handsome narrow lips pressed tightly together.
Then he began to recite a torrent of extracts memor-
ised from French conversation pieces, raising his hand
somewhat preciously to his brow, a gesture he
employed with special predilection on the stage. The
woman was enraptured. Not since her girlhood had
she encountered such an agreeable and gracious young
man. How refreshing, how polished, how bohemian,
and yet how courteous! She made a point of expressing
her delight at having finally made his acquaintance. At
this the actor sprang to his feet, gave a low, almost
over-theatrical bow, and replied that, on the contrary,

it was he who'd had the good fortune to meet such a genteel and distinguished lady.

At the opposite end of the table the men talked politics. They spoke of state delegations, constitutional crises and of Prime Minister Kálmán Széll.

'Ah, yes,' Környey sighed. 'A visionary statesman and a first-rate brain.'

Priboczay, who was an old forty-eighter, became visibly heated.

'No doubt because he went to Vienna for the unveiling of the Albrecht statue. He, prime minister of Hungary. For shame!'

'Tactics,' Környey replied.

'Tactics,' Priboczay nodded bitterly. 'And when they ordered our boys out to the Hentzi statue in Pest? That was tactics too, I suppose? Bánffy would never have done such a thing. Never. Your man's a common toady.'

'*Raison d'état*,' Feri Füzes commented.

Now Priboczay was really fuming.

'Right, Law and Justice? Isn't that the party slogan?' he hollered to provoke the young government supporter. 'Schwarzgelb mercenary, Viennese lackey!'

Feri Füzes could not allow the Hungarian prime minister's name to be slandered in this fashion. Enough was enough. As a man with an almost superstitious deference towards all figures of authority, he ventured to reply:

'And what of your famous Ferenc Kossuth? I suppose he's going to hand us a free-trade zone on a platter? Together with Hungarian supremacy?'

'You leave him out of this. He's the son of our great father Kossuth. You wouldn't understand such things, my boy.'

Feri Füzes blushed. Then, with a certain peevish superiority he observed:

'I have every respect for Lajos Kossuth and his politics. But just like everyone else, Lajos Kossuth has his good points and his bad points.'

And he looked about him for support.

But at this everyone had chuckled, including Környey, and even the oldest and staunchest of sixty-seveners, for they all knew that Feri Füzes, although the perfect gentleman, had less than his fair share of grey matter.

For a moment Feri Füzes was at a complete loss. Then he asked himself how such behaviour could possibly offend a proper gentleman, and looked for someone else to provoke. But the others soon placated him and he went on smiling his familiar smile.

Ákos did not take part in the debate. What did he care for either Kálmán Széll or Ferenc Kossuth? Weightier concerns and deeper questions played upon his mind.

He sat immersed in his own thoughts, his morning dreams still swimming through his head, his face heavily shadowed by his own bad conscience. He glanced towards his wife, who was already eating.

Seeing this, he appeared to reach a momentous decision. He frowned, put on his spectacles and plunged into a fastidious study of the menu.

He couldn't see it too clearly because, in places, the

ink of the hectograph had smudged and faded. He reached into his upper waistcoat pocket for the magnifying glass he normally reserved for deciphering *litterae armales*, and, the strength of his spectacles thus doubled, examined the menu in detail.

Applying no less rigour and self-sacrificing passion to the study of this document than to the search for some sixteenth-century Vajkay of Bozsó whose descent remained uncertain, he scoured the family tree of noble dishes for the entry he had been dreaming of unceasingly since the day before. On this occasion it was between the stuffed sirloin and the pork chops that the name 'goulash' humbly but meaningfully stood. No sooner had he hit upon it with his finger than the waiter set it down before him.

'Smells delicious,' commented Feri Füzes.

The comment annoyed Ákos. What had it to do with Feri Füzes how the goulash smelled? Ákos would decide for himself. And with that he lowered his gristly, pale, almost cadaverous nose towards the red liquid in the silver bowl, steeping himself in the dizzying delight of inhaling the goulash's fragrant vapours deep into his lungs. Feri Füzes was quite right, it really did smell superb. And as for the taste! It was simply indescribable.

He devoured the goulash greedily, polishing his plate with squares of bread, just as Weisz and Partner had done the day before.

'Ilonka,' the Panthers called out, 'over here! More rolls, more croissants.'

And along came Ilonka, the owner's fifteen-year-old

daughter, who filled the empty wicker baskets with rolls and pastries. She sauntered around her father's establishment, her head filled with hopeless theatrical dreams. She wanted to be an actress and tread the boards of Sárszeg's Kisfaludy Theatre. She spoke to no one of her secret ambition, only gazed incessantly at Imre Zányi, longingly, silently, unhappily, sighing as she passed him on her way to the next table. She was as pale as a damp bread roll.

'What'll you drink?' asked Környey.

'Forgive me,' said Ákos, 'but not a drop has passed my lips in fifteen years.'

Szunyogh pricked up his ears.

'But a dish like that,' the commander in chief urged, 'cries out for lubrication. Come on, old chap, just the one glass.'

'Perhaps a sip of beer,' said Vajkay, casting a quizzical glance at Gál, his family physician. 'Less alcohol. I'll have a glass of beer,' he called to the wine steward. Then, as an afterthought: 'The smallest glass you have.'

Ákos took a couple of temperate sips, the white foam clinging to his grey moustache. This he sucked into his mouth and swallowed.

Then he ordered breast of veal, followed by vanilla noodles, which, luckily for him, were still on the menu, and were excellent. Then he ordered cheese – Emmenthal – and two apples to finish.

'Won't it disagree with you, Father?' his wife interrupted at one point with a smiling reproach. She was still being entertained by the actor and the pharmacist.

'Of course not,' the others replied, including Dr Gál.

'Another glass of beer,' they proposed with gusto.

'That was plenty,' Ákos protested. 'A veritable Lucullan luncheon,' he added with a chuckle and felt that his meagre stomach was now quite bloated.

From his inside pocket, Bálint Környey took out a silver cigar case with an elegant engraving of a gun dog adorning its lid. He pulled down the leather flap separating the two rows of cigars and, without a word, set the case down before Ákos.

Ákos took a splendid dark Tisza cigar, tore off the band and, without waiting for the comedian to hand him his pocket knife, bit off the end. Szolyvay at once supplied him with a light.

Observing this, his wife's jaw dropped a little, but even Dr Gál seemed reluctant to dampen Ákos's spirits and, without the slightest protestation, continued talking to his friends.

The old man sucked at his cigar with all the voraciousness of a baby at the breast, the succulent, bitter teat glistening with his spittle. The smoke caressed his long-chastened palate, the familiar fragrance tickling his nose, overpowering his brain, soothing his ancient, torpid blood and stirring long-forgotten sensations within him. What did he care for the chatter that surrounded him? For constitutional law, for Viennese intrigues, for Dreyfus or Labori? He leaned back into his chair and began digesting.

Later, however, he too ventured the odd remark. He spoke mostly to wise old Szunyogh, who, like a deep-sea diver, brought to the conversation a wealth of treasures from the depths of his enormous erudition, which by now lay long submerged beneath a sea of wine and schnapps, including a few choice remarks on the medieval Latin of royal letters of donation, which interested Ákos. Enveloped in a cloud of smoke, the gathering huddled warmly together. The restaurant was now all but empty. Only they entertained no thoughts of going home.

It was half past three when a middle-aged man in a grubby, soft-blue shirt and a worn, smoke-coloured overcoat appeared, who didn't belong to this gentlemanly gathering.

'Your most humble servant,' he whined by way of greeting, bowing like a Gypsy.

The others addressed him in the familiar form and immediately invited him to sit down.

He was Arácsy, director of the Kisfaludy Theatre. He clasped an umbrella in his hand, which, even on fine days like these, he always carried with him, perhaps to inspire pity, perhaps to evoke the trusty staffs with which the nation's journeymen, the actors, beat the highway on their endless travels. He constantly complained of gloom and doom, and his voice, which had once declaimed the tribulations of stage heroes, was now no more than a plaintive whimper. Who would have thought he owned a pretty little house in Sárszeg and a pretty little vineyard out of town? Not to mention a tidy sum in the Agricultural Bank.

A half-hour visit to the King of Hungary after lunch and a friendly chat with the good gentlemen of Sárszeg formed part of his daily round. Noticing Ákos, he immediately set to work on the new acquaintance.

Assuming the most modest and friendly of smiles, he expressed his amazement at having as yet been denied the honour of seeing Ákos at the theatre.

'I'm afraid we lead a rather quiet life,' said Ákos, turning to stare into space, 'in our humble home.'

'But I sincerely hope you will now do us the honour,' said the theatre director, placing a pink theatre ticket on the table before Ákos.

It was for a box in the stalls.

'I don't know,' said Ákos, glancing at his wife.

The table fell silent. Husband and wife conferred.

'You see,' said the woman blushing, 'we don't usually go to the theatre,' and she gave a peculiar shrug of her shoulders.

At this Imre Zányi piped up:

'We'd be honoured, my dear lady.'

'When is it for?' asked Mrs Vajkay.

'Tomorrow evening,' the leading man was quick to reply. 'What is it we're playing?'

'*The Geisha*,' said Szolyvay, who played the part of Wun-Hi to rapturous applause.

'A splendid piece,' Kornyey roared. 'Superb music. Haven't you seen it?'

'No.'

'Much better than *The Blue Lady* or that fashionable new operetta, *Shulamit*.'

'The Jewish operetta?' asked Feri Füzes with a sneer.

'That's the one,' said Környey with a nod of the head. 'I'll be there myself.'

'Surely you won't turn me down?' said the director, blinking affectedly at the woman and turning out his palms in ham despair.

'Let's go, Father.'

'I'm yours to command,' Ákos said with a jocularity that did not suit him and was thoroughly alien to his nature. The others were amused. With a theatrical sweep of the hand he snatched up the ticket and stuffed it in his pocket.

'Devil take it, we'll go. Thank you kindly.'

In the street, they did not discuss the day's events. Not the lunch, nor the beer, nor the cigar. Their thoughts were preoccupied with the theatrical performance they were to witness the following evening.

At one corner they came across a playbill in a wooden frame, hanging from the wall on a length of rusty wire. Here they came to a halt.

They studied the playbill carefully:

THE GEISHA
or the tale of a Japanese tearoom

Musical Comedy in Three Acts

Libretto: Owen Hall. Music: Sidney Jones

Translated by Béla Fáy and Emil Makkai

Commences: 7.30 p.m. Ends: after 10.

Zányi wasn't among the cast, which disappointed them. Only Szolyvay. The other actors they did not know.

VI

---

in which the Vajkays attend the Sárszeg performance of The Geisha

On Monday afternoon they were talking.
'But you really must have a haircut, Father.'
'Why?'
'You can't go to the theatre like that. Look how matted it is – at the back and at the sides.'

Ákos's hair was thinning only on top. At the sides his hoary curls sprang thick and wild. He had last visited the barber in the spring. Since then his hair had grown tousled and unkempt. Dandruff dusted the lapels of his jacket.

'Come into town with me,' said the woman. 'I have to call on Weisz and Partner anyway. I want to buy a handbag. I've nowhere to put my opera glasses.'

Ákos accompanied his wife to the leather-goods store. Mr Weisz served them in person.

Before them on the counter he lined up his splendid wares, recently arrived from England. They inspected the brand-new suitcases, marvelling at how easily they opened and closed. They could certainly do with new suitcases themselves, but for now they had only come about the crocodile handbag in the window.

Mr Weisz gestured to a sickly, sorry figure who sat buried among trade catalogues in a glass cage lit by butterfly lamps. He emerged, scurried over to the window display, fetched the handbag, and then, after climbing a ladder to lift down more new bags, made some inaudible comment in his plaintive, nasal voice. He was the Partner, the unsung, neglected talent whose name nobody knew. The signs of some incurable gastric disorder were written all over his sour face. Clearly he didn't eat the same goulash as Mr Weisz.

They spent a long time haggling over the leather handbag. It was expensive, nine forints, and they only managed to reduce it to 8.50. But it was worth the money. The woman hurried it home at once.

Ákos turned into Gombkötő Street, to the barber's.

The barber gave Ákos the full treatment. He wrapped him in a towel and lathered his face with tepid foam. With the bib around his chest, Ákos looked like a little boy treated to cakes at a patisserie, his face smeared thick with whipped cream.

When his assistant had finished the shaving, the barber set about the old man's hair, shaping it on top with electric clippers, scraping away any leftover stubble behind the ears with an open blade, then trimming, raking, combing and smoothing the sides. He carefully snipped the grey tufts of hair from Ákos's ears and spread his moustache with fine twirling wax. This had just arrived from Tiszaújlak and, at seven kreuzers a tub, possessed the singular property of bonding even the most stubborn of Magyar moustaches. Finally, when he had swept away any remaining strands of fallen hair, he dusted Ákos's temples with a soft brush and pressed his hair into shape with a net.

When net and towel were finally removed, Ákos replaced the copy of *Saucy Simon* in which he had read many mischievous stories from the pen of some amateur scribbler, and looked into the mirror. His face darkened a little.

He hardly recognised himself.

A new man sat on the velvet cushions of the barber's swivel chair. His hair, although it had just been cut, seemed more bounteous than before. His moustache curled into a sharp and utterly unfamiliar fork, blackened by the Tiszaújlak wax, and as bright and stiff as if hammered from cast iron. His chin, on the other hand, was smooth, fresh and velvety. Every pore seemed younger. But different, too, and this unsettled him.

He examined himself mistrustfully with his small watery eyes. He simply couldn't get used to the unfamiliar expression his face now wore.

The barber noticed this.

'Will that be all?'

'Yes, that's fine,' Ákos mumbled in a voice that seemed to say the opposite.

He paid, took his cane and looked once more into the mirror. And now he saw that his face was red, too, and even a little fatter. Yes, decidedly redder and fatter.

His wife was well satisfied.

She too was doing her hair, and had just lit the spirit lamp on her dressing table where she placed her curling irons. She crimped the thin strands of hair on her forehead, more out of etiquette than vanity; that was simply what one did. She powdered her face but, her eyesight being weak, she had difficulty applying the powder evenly from the chamois. Here and there small floury patches remained on her skin. Into her hands, chapped from needlework, she rubbed a drop or two of glycerine. Then she went to look out her one and only festive dress.

This hung from the last hanger in her wardrobe, covered with a sheet. She would take it out only once or twice a year, for Easter, Corpus Christi or some similar occasion. Thus, in spite of having been made so many years before, the dress still looked as good as new.

It was made of lilac silk with black lace trimmings and white lace frills at the neck. It had leg of mutton sleeves and skirts that reached the ground. With it went a pair of elbow-length gloves. She pinned a gold brooch to her breast and hung diamond earrings from her ears – the family jewellery she had inherited from her mother. Into her new crocodile handbag she slipped her mother-of-pearl opera glasses and a lorgnette she had once bought as a present for Skylark, but which they always shared.

Ákos dressed ponderously. With him, dressing was

always a trial. His wife had laid out his clothes for him, but still, to his vexation, he couldn't find this or that. He had trouble fastening his collar, then two buttons broke one after the other on his starched shirt front and he couldn't find his tie. At first he found his frock coat too loose, then too tight, and he longed to be back in his mouse-grey jacket. When he was finally dressed, however, and stood beside his wife, he was not displeased with his appearance. His silver wedding came to mind, when they had both set off to the photographer's. He looked fresh, refined and gentlemanly. Only his somewhat disrespectful expression troubled him, which he had already noticed at the barber's. In vain had he washed and brushed his hair, it simply wouldn't go away. His moustache seemed to rear higher and higher. If he pressed it down, it immediately sprang up again.

The Kisfaludy Theatre was housed in one of the tallest buildings in Sárszeg, at least half of which was occupied by the Széchenyi Inn and Café, with a ballroom upstairs. The rest belonged to the theatre, one entrance of which opened out on to a small side street.

Here the Vajkays slipped into the foyer to escape unnecessary attention, and from there to their twoseater box in the stalls. The usher opened the door for them and pressed a programme into their hands.

The woman sat down at the front. She opened the programme, which was hardly bigger than a lady's handkerchief, and skimmed through it. For a while Ákos hovered in the background, observing the musicians as they leafed through their scores and tuned their instruments in the orchestra pit, which receded into the cellar directly beneath him. The lamplight struck the white forehead of the flautist. The violinists were chatting in German. A Czech tuba player with an apoplectic red face and a minuscule nose, who was known to perform at funeral processions, was just raising his serpentine instrument to his neck as if struggling in a fit of suffocation with a golden octopus.

Although the audience was still sparse, a stifling atmosphere already hung over the auditorium. On Sunday there had been two performances, a matinee and an evening show, and the steamy vapours of their passing storm lingered thick and oppressive in the air. The dark recesses of the boxes were still strewn with discarded tickets, scattered sweet wrappers and scraps of hardening orange peel. The theatre had been neither swept nor aired. Furthermore, to the eternal shame of Sárszeg's only theatre – and in spite of countless impassioned pleas in the local press – electric lighting had still not been introduced in the auditorium, and the old oil lamps continued to emit their layers of heavy smoke and a certain melancholy odour, referred to by the locals as 'stage stench'.

It was above all for this reason that Skylark never went to the theatre. As soon as she inhaled this air, felt its heat strike her face, and saw the unfamiliar sight of seething crowds before and beneath her, her head would spin and she'd be overcome by a sort of nausea that resembled seasickness. On the one occasion when they had booked three seats in the stalls, they were forced to go home in the middle of the first act. Since then they hadn't been to the theatre at all. Their daughter said she'd rather stay at home with her needlework.

Gradually the auditorium came to life.

Opposite, in a circle box, sat the Priboczays – the mother a good-natured, fair-haired creature, the father an exemplary paterfamilias, and their four daughters who all wore their hair in exactly the same fashion, parted neatly in the middle, and all wore the same pink dresses. Like four pink roses in varying stages of bloom.

Beside them sat Judge Doba with his wife, a lean, dark-haired, flirtatious woman who simply lived for the theatre, or rather for the actors. She always dragged her husband along with her, who would sit with his prematurely bald head buried miserably and wearily in his hands.

The judge was a very melancholy man, and not without good reason. His wife betrayed him left and right, quite openly, with actors, articled clerks and even older grammar-school boys. It was said she'd had separate door keys made for her lovers, who would visit her whenever her husband was not at home. Doba for his part knew nothing, absolutely nothing – or at least didn't show it. In court he would excel himself in the execution of his lofty office, impartially administering justice to others. But at the end of the day he'd sit in the Széchenyi Café with his wife and her circle, light up a Virginia and keep silence. Now he was silent too.

Leaning out of the club box sat Feri Füzes and Galló with a host of aldermen and other town dignitaries, who made up the membership of the Theatre Committee. They all suddenly rose to their feet. Gyalokay had arrived, the new Lord Lieutenant of Prime Minister Kálmán Széll.

Gyalokay really did appear to be the 'agile' figure who was often described in the *Sárszeg Gazette*. He had nimble quicksilver movements and a bushy, chaotically upward-shooting moustache which was so dense one could have been forgiven for imagining the Lord Lieutenant had inadvertently left his whisker brush in its midst – two thick whisker brushes poking up from the two separate stems of his moustache. He simply couldn't stop fidgeting, waving and bowing, springing up from his seat every other minute as if it had turned to hot coals beneath him. He reminded one of some feverish, restless rodent – of an otter, above all.

He had hardly finished with the gentlemen in the club box when he turned to nod a greeting to the Vajkays, at which Ákos emerged from the shadows and gave a deep bow. The audience switched their opera glasses between Vajkay and the Lord Lieutenant. Fortunately they were soon forced to conclude their alternating inspection, for the conductor tapped his baton and the orchestra launched into the overture.

Many were already familiar with the pleasing melodies of *The Geisha*. There were some, the Priboczay girls for example, who had already seen the whole performance several times and knew the songs by heart. Indeed, all four girls had learned to play them on the piano. For Ákos, on the other hand, everything was strange and new. Not only the audience, but the illuminated stage front and even the curtain with its embroidered mask from whose open mouth a quill protruded like a lolling tongue.

As the curtain rose, his eyes and mouth gaped open. He leaned forward to focus all his attention on the stage. The fantasy world of eastern legend came to life before him. Flashes of yellow, red, green and lilac; colours merging with movements, sounds and words, new and unfamiliar sensations fusing with ancient, half-forgotten reveries.

It was all quite dazzling.

The façade of a Japanese tearoom, lanterns swaying against the indigo sky backdrop, and the tiny tearoom girls, the geishas singing in splendid unison.

His ears were struck by snatches of words:

> Happy Japan,
> Garden of glitter!
> Flower and fan
> Flutter and flitter . . .
> Merry little geishas we!
> Come along at once and see
> Ample entertainment free,
> Given as you take your tea.

'Japan,' he whispered to his wife.

'Yes, Japan. Japan.'

They could not entirely follow the performance. The events that passed on stage, the various happenings in time and space, became jumbled before them into a decorative skein whose strands and fibres they were unable to unravel at once. The woman ran her finger down the programme, reading the names of the chorus girls – names like Márta Virág, Anny Joó, Teréz Feledy, Lenke Labancz.

Singing could now also be heard from the wings, still to the tune of the ensemble. The audience listened to the invisible singer who made a sudden and sonorous entrance on stage, at which the auditorium erupted in applause. A huge bouquet was handed up from the orchestra, which the new arrival, the leading geisha, swept up to stage level with a bow, then set to one side. She was Olga Orosz, the prima donna, the infamous, the celebrated, the fascinating star of the theatre about whom there was always so much gossip.

Ákos asked his wife for the opera glasses. The prima donna soon fitted into the two swollen crystal circles of the lenses.

She was playing Mimosa, the leading singer of the tearoom, who was, like all the other girls, in the business of love. This, according to the Japanese custom, was not to be seen as something degrading: she earned an honest living through the sale of her body. She was dressed in a full and flowery kimono with white silk slippers. She wore her hair Mimosa-style, with carnations gracefully pinned on either side. Under the dark vault of her eyebrows, her almond eyes flickered hesitantly up at Ákos.

In the strange stage lighting, it was, even with the aid of opera glasses, quite impossible to tell whether her eyes were black or blue. At times they really did appear jet black, then blue again, but for the most part they were somewhere between the two, sparkling in flashes of violet light. She may even have been a touch cross-eyed. If so, this suited her all the more.

And her expression was intriguing, too. She appeared to look into everybody's eyes at once, addressing herself to each gaze individually, trying to bewitch each one with the same empty, superficial charm. To say she had a beautiful voice would be to go too far. Her voice was muted, faint, veiled. When she switched to ordinary speech she let out a husky giggle at the end of every phrase. They said she was a heavy smoker and drank too much, which would explain the hoarseness.

Ákos was not interested in the plot, having little time for stories forged by the imagination. As a heraldist, a scholar of blazonry, he insisted on historical veracity. He didn't consider novels and plays as things to be taken 'seriously'. He wouldn't even look at a work on which imagination had left its magic mark. In his younger days he had attempted one or two, but had soon wearied of them. Whenever books were discussed in company, he'd always remark that he only read 'as much as the exigencies of his vocation would allow'. As the 'exigencies of his vocation' allowed very little, he read nothing at all.

He did once take a careful look at Smith's book on character. This he praised highly and for a long time recommended to his friends. As a rule he preferred stimulating, edifying books which elucidated some moral truth or the interconnections between otherwise meaningless or incomprehensible facts. Truths like 'hard work is always rewarded' or 'evil never goes unpunished'; books that rock one in the lap of the comforting illusion that no one suffers undeservingly in this world, nor dies of stomach cancer without due cause. But where were the interconnections here?

Reginald Fairfax, the English sea captain played by a tall and slender young actor, kissed Mimosa full on the mouth.

The woman offered no resistance. Divesting herself of all the nobility of her sex, she herself offered the European stranger her lips and proceeded to instruct him in the art of love.

Mimosa would not let go of the youth, holding him in a brazen embrace. This woman knew no shame at all. The two mouths remained glued together for some time, devouring each other, tearing at each other, drinking in delight, refusing to break asunder. The smouldering embrace grew still more passionate, while the good citizens of Sárszeg waited breathlessly for what should follow, their eyes riveted to the couple, watching, learning, like children at school, thinking of how they too, in similar circumstances, would do exactly the same.

The glasses brought this image so close to Ákos that for a moment he shrank back.

He put the glasses down disapprovingly, frowned, then glanced at his wife as if to ask what she thought of this unsightly scene.

The woman said nothing. She had long held a rather damning opinion of actors. She often spoke of Etel Pifkó, an ancient local actress who had poisoned herself while pregnant and whose grave lay beyond the walls of Sárszeg cemetery because she had not been buried in consecrated ground and hadn't enjoyed the Church's final blessing.

Wun-Hi lightened the couple's spirits. This pigtailed Chinaman, owner of the Tea House of Ten Thousand Joys, went dashing busily to and fro. His powers of invention knew no bounds.

'You know who that is, don't you?' whispered Ákos.

'Who?'

'Szolyvay.'

'Never!'

'Look at the programme.'

'Goodness, I'd never have recognised him. What an excellent disguise!'

'And the voice too, the voice. Just listen to it. Totally unrecognisable.'

Szolyvay lisped and hawked and bleated. After his every prank the Vajkays looked at each other, their smiles spreading wider each time.

When Marquis Imari appeared beneath a red parasol, threatening to put Wun-Hi's tearoom up for auction, the panic-stricken Chinaman immediately threw himself at the marquis's feet. The whole theatre erupted in a roar of laughter. Ákos and his wife laughed too.

They laughed so much that they didn't hear a knock at the door behind them. Környey came into their box; the first act was nearly over.

'Well,' he inquired, 'enjoying yourselves?'

'Tremendously,' the woman replied.

'Amusing stuff and nonsense,' said Ákos, tempering his response. 'Entertaining, at any rate.'

'Just you wait; the best is still to come.'

Környey, true theatre buff that he was, only used his opera glasses to observe the audience.

'Look up there,' he said.

He pointed to a box in the upper circle where Imre Zányi sat in the company of a shady-looking woman with straw-blonde hair.

'He sits there every evening,' said the commander in chief pointing up at Zányi. 'But only when *she*'s playing. The great *she*, Olga Orosz. He's madly in love with her, you know. Has been for two years.'

Ákos focused his opera glasses alternately on Zányi and Olga Orosz. His eyes couldn't seem to get enough of them.

During the interval Környey entertained Mrs Vajkay with local gossip, while Ákos, in his serious frock coat, neatly combed hair and waxed moustache, made an appearance in the club box before the gentlemen of Sárszeg. He paid his respects to the Lord Lieutenant, who received him very warmly, his light, fidgety body leaping out from, and back into, his seat in a flash. He immediately invited Ákos to join him for lunch the following day, when the Budapest commissioner would also be present. Then they began to discourse on the proper conduct of elections, so freely and in such depth that they failed to notice that the second act had already begun. This Ákos watched in their company from beginning to end.

Miklós Ijas arrived halfway through the act, having

only just completed his editorial duties. He sat down in the seat permanently reserved for the *Sárszeg Gazette*. As always, he didn't cast a single glance at the stage. He rested his head on the back of the seat before him in a gesture that seemed to say: rubbish. He was never satisfied with the performance, yet never missed a single one. He was especially critical of Szolyvay, of whom he'd recently written: 'He plays to the gallery and his Wun-Hi is an altogether scandalous example of provincial histrionics, totally lacking in either character or conscience, which would be summarily dismissed by any self-respecting audience in Pest.'

This judgement, which caused no small stir, was considered too harsh by many and entirely unjust by others, including Szolyvay himself, who, after a few days' contemplation, reverted to his tried and tested theatrical antics which never failed to bring irresistible hoots of laughter from his audience. The editor pursed his lips in vexation.

Ijas only raised his head when Margit Lator came on stage, playing the part of Miss Molly Seamore. She was, in his eyes, a genuine actress, and in his reviews he praised her refreshing ingenuity, rated her vocal range superior to that of Olga Orosz, compared her to the legendary Klára Küry, and repeatedly insisted that she belonged on the Budapest stage. Some said that all the poems he published in the *Sárszeg Gazette* were dedicated to her.

At the end of the second act, Környey went over to the club box and took Ákos down to the courtyard to smoke a cigarette.

They groped and zigzagged their way through dimly lit archways until they reached the first floor of the inn, with its red marble stairway whose wide steps Ákos had once climbed with his wife and daughter to the ballroom above. The large mirror, before which women would make final adjustments to their coiffures before entering the ball, still stood between two cypress trees. But now the ballroom door was firmly locked. A cold, unfriendly twilight hung in the corridor. The chambermaid, a plump woman in white stockings and high-heeled patent-leather shoes, leaned on the banisters, rocking back and forth with a copper candlestick holder in her hand, making unmistakable gestures to the young men on the floor below. Something indecent was evidently afoot.

They hurried past her down the steps and out through a little door into the theatre courtyard. Here they lit up.

Acetylene lamps illuminated the canvas backs of the stage sets with a garish glow. Seedy youths took down the lanterns which had been used on stage and carried them to the props cupboard. In the middle of the courtyard, beneath a large sycamore, sat Szolyvay at a one-time restaurant table drinking a spritzer.

'You were splendid,' said Környey, complimenting him.

'Splendid,' Ákos echoed, 'absolutely splendid.' And he chuckled.

He wrung his hands continually as he stood gazing at the actor, chuckling. A devil of a fellow, this Szolyvay. Szolyvay, yet not Szolyvay. The pigtail was still swinging from his bare head and beads of perspiration rolled across his thick make-up. Ákos could not contain his laughter.

Szolyvay was preoccupied with graver matters, deep in conversation with the group that surrounded him concerning the latest developments in the old affair between Olga Orosz and Imre Zányi.

Dr Gál was also present, as the theatre's in-house physician, together with several members of the Theatre Committee and other insiders and friends of the performers. Among them stood Papa Fehér, manager of the Agricultural Bank. For want of anyone better, he had his arms around an anonymous-looking geisha girl with large dark-blue shadows on her eyelids.

'It was a frightful scandal,' said the comedian, picking up where he had left off. 'Last night we began Act Three of *The Cardinal* half an hour late. The audience didn't know what had happened, but it was that madman Zányi. After the second act, he'd set off into town just as he was, in a purple robe and golden chain, and burst into Olga Orosz's flat in Bólyai Street. Seized by a sudden fit of jealousy, he smashed one of her windows, made an almighty racket and came back with a bloody fist. They saw him from the window of the Széchenyi too, pulling his purple cardinal's robe up round his knees as he ran back to the theatre. It was quite a scene, I can tell you. It'll cost him a month's pay.' The others were dumbstruck and pressed for further details.

'Olga will have nothing more to do with him,'

Szolyvay continued. 'She's getting married. They say Dani Kárász has asked for her hand.'

So Dani Kárász, the son of the wealthy landowner István Kárász, was going to marry an actress. This excited them. They were hungry for more, but the comedian threw down his cigarette when he saw Miklós Ijas coming towards them from Margit Lator's dresser. They hadn't spoken since the appearance of his review. With all the dignity of a mandarin, Szolyvay withdrew.

Környey caught Ijas by the arm and introduced him to Ákos.

'I don't believe you've met,' he said. 'Ákos Vajkay; Editor Ijas.'

Ijas pouted. He objected to being addressed in this fashion.

He bowed and raised his hat to Ákos.

'How do you do,' said Ákos.

'How do you do,' said Ijas.

They walked as far as the patisserie together, sizing each other up, but without uttering a word. There they parted.

Ákos bought a box of chocolates wrapped in gold ribbon and took it up to his wife's box.

His head was swimming from all he had seen and heard. He hadn't really understood it all, there was simply too much to take in. He gazed bemused into thin air, and was relieved when the curtain rose and he could sink back into the artificial, but at least more transparent, spectacle of the play.

The geishas, now dressed as bridesmaids, celebrated

with song and dance Marquis Imari's wedding day, among them the girl whom Papa Fehér had been holding in his arms. All the little misses, fair and dark, fat and thin, turned their pretty snouts towards the gorgeous spectacle.

Among them, commanding centre stage, stood Olga Orosz, soaring from triumph to triumph. All the action on stage seemed to revolve about her. She was the focus of every word and every gaze. And what a beautiful creature she was, too, what a wicked, godless little kitten! She wasn't even young any more. Past thirty, for sure, perhaps even over thirty-five. But her flesh was powdery and voluptuously weary, as if tenderised by all the different beds and arms in which it had lain. Her face was as soft as the pulpy flesh of an overripe banana, her breasts like two tiny bunches of grapes. She exuded a certain seedy charm, a poetry of premature corruption and decay. She breathed the air as if it burned her palate, baking her small, hot, whorish mouth. It was as if she were sucking a sweet or slurping champagne.

She hardly sang at all, only trilled and screeched the notes of some haphazard scale. But the audience were riveted. They would have thrown their very souls at her feet.

Is there no justice? Upon the head of this abomination, this lecherous, almost biblical fornicator, surely sulphurous rains should fall? Instead she was swamped with flowers. Everyone knew all the details of her immoral existence and that her very soul was up for sale. They knew she belonged to the dregs of society, a filthy rag not even fit to wipe one's boots on. But what did they care? They worshipped her, idolised her, prized her above gentleness and kindness, she who was worthy neither of love nor respect, who scoffed at all things beautiful and sublime. No justice, no justice!

Pressing his opera glasses to his eyes, Ákos wondered what he would do if he ever met her. Turn away perhaps, or measure her with a scathing stare, or simply spit on the ground in front of her?

From these dark thoughts it was once again Wun-Hi who distracted him, dancing out on to the centre of the stage and this time really surpassing himself. Fanning his face with his long pigtail, he launched into the famous vaudeville song:

> Chin Chin Chinaman
> Muchee muchee sad!
> He afraid allo trade
> Wellee wellee bad!
> Noee joke, brokee broke
> Makee shutee shop!
> Chin Chin Chinaman,
> Chop, chop, chop!

The effect was so great that the show was held up for several minutes as the applause refused to abate.

It came from everywhere, from the boxes, the stalls and the gods. Leaning right out of his box and completely forgetting himself, Ákos was clapping too, melting, utterly bewitched, into this rapture of approval, and hammering out the rhythm of the ditty on the sill of his box. He no longer cared whose glasses were focused upon him. He was swept along by the fever of the crowd, as was his wife. They laughed so much that tears streamed down their faces.

'Chin Chin Chinaman . . .' the woman chortled.

'Chop, chop, chop,' Ákos echoed playfully, pointing back at her, slicing the air with his finger.

But there was more to come. Now it was time for the topical stanzas of the song, clumsily adapted to reflect the local political issues of the day. Sárszeg was also 'wellee, wellee bad', because it was a sea of mud, had no sewage system and its theatre ran without electricity. The audience roared.

The Lord Lieutenant, himself implicated by the joke, none the less tried to set an appropriate example by graciously condescending to beat his palms together to show that he appreciated the severe, but not unjust, criticism of the general state of affairs.

He only sprang to his feet – and then like a jack-in-the-box – when it was suggested that the Hentzi statue was also for the 'chop, chop, chop'. At this he withdrew to the depths of his box. As the representative of the Hungarian government of the day there was, after all, little else he could do.

In this highly charged atmosphere the show came to a close. Ákos registered to his surprise that the curtain had fallen for the last time and the audience was already thronging towards the cloakroom.

For a few moments he remained in his seat studying the programme and rubbing the sweat from his palms. He took his neatly folded handkerchief from his frock-coat pocket and wiped his burning face. The woman searched under the box seats for her handbag.

By the time they reached the foyer, the crowd had thinned.

Arácsy, standing before the box office, gave Ákos a thoroughly unctuous greeting and squeezed his hand. Ákos expressed his enthusiasm for the performance and promised they would come again. But then the stage door opened and the prima donna came running over to the director.

Without even removing her make-up, she had merely slipped on a light silk gown and was ready to hurry off somewhere.

The old man looked at her hesitantly.

Arácsy introduced her.

Ákos bowed before the prima donna no less courteously than he had bowed before the Lord Lieutenant at the beginning of the evening.

The woman offered her hand and Ákos took it.

'Congratulations,' he stuttered, 'You were magnificent.'

'Oh, I hardly think so,' replied the prima donna, feigning modesty.

'Truly, madam, truly you were. And I am not one for flattery. You were quite magnificent.'

'Really?' lisped Olga Orosz, letting out a husky chuckle.

An overpowering fragrance wafted about her, the latest perfume, Heliotrope.

The warm, soft little paw would not let go of the man's hand. Not until some moments had passed.

Ákos went back over to his wife who was waiting by the exit.

'The way she laughs,' the woman remarked. 'Just like on stage.'

'Yes, she plays her part quite naturally.'

They strolled through the still warm night. Only when they reached Széchenyi Square did the woman speak:

'They say she's in love with Zányi.'

'No,' replied Ákos. 'She's in love with Dani Kárász. She's going to marry him.'

At that moment an open landau thundered past them, drawn by two splendid, lively bays. Inside, pressed close together, sat Olga Orosz and Dani Kárász.

The old couple watched the carriage disappear.

VII

—————

in which the couple talk to a fledgling provincial poet

At midday on Tuesday their table at the King of Hungary, which the waiter had reserved for them, remained empty.

Ákos ate with the Lord Lieutenant. His wife took the opportunity to lunch with an old friend, Mrs Záhoczky, the widow of a colonel and the president of the Catholic Ladies' Association, at whose home the ladies of Sárszeg would congregate every Tuesday to discuss, over coffee and whipped cream, preserves and assorted pastries, matters of everyday business.

Lately they had proved themselves particularly zealous in the charitable field. They had founded an orphanage, a Mary Society for young ladies, and a Martha Home for serving girls, where one could be assured of finding reliable staff. Their attention had even extended to the rapid spread of poverty in the town, and they provided free meals and clothes to a number of the poor, quite irrespective of religion. All their members made sacrifices, each according to her means, and they were looked upon with gratitude by the whole town.

Mrs Vajkay's husband came for his wife at around six o'clock. He related to her all that had occurred at the Lord Lieutenant's lunch.

There must have been about forty people present, he said, among them the Budapest commissioner, a most obliging gentleman. They had all had a splendid time. The consommé was served in little cups, not in bowls as at home or at the King of Hungary. There were two types of fish, followed by fillet steak in a sauce with ham dumplings. There had been a choice of dessert, which he had found himself too full to try. He had, however, allowed himself half a glass of French champagne.

His wife, for her part, described the afternoon tea. Above all she extolled the milk loaf, which was particularly fresh and spongy.

On the corner of Széchenyi Square they ran into Miklós Ijas.

Everyone ran into someone in Sárszeg, like it or not, several times a day. For the town was so constructed that wherever one was headed, one's route unavoidably led across the square. The townsfolk hardly bothered to greet one another, and merely signalled with their eyes. Such encounters were not occasions of any great excitement. It was rather like members of the same large family meeting one another in the hall of their own home.

The only point of interest was the time at which such encounters would occur. Everyone kept his own hours. Mályvády, for example, would always come striding across the square at exactly half past seven, followed by his pupils, to whom he was as friendly and benign out of school as he was strict once the first bell had sounded. His pupils stumbled behind him carrying cardboard boxes, discs and iron rods for their physics experiments. Sometimes they could even be seen bringing tame rabbits or sparrows which their teacher would place inside a bell jar, deprive of air and summarily execute. Szunyogh would appear just after eight and, hearing the little school bell announce the commencement of classes, would often break into a run, struggling in his overcoat which he wore with the collar turned up, for he was terrified of the headmaster and did not care to be seen arriving late. At nine Dr Gál would make his first appearance. At ten Priboczay completed his familiar manicural manoeuvres outside the pharmacy. At eleven Környey would pass in the driving seat of a light gig, whisked along by a strong, iron-grey horse, belonging to the fire brigade. Just before twelve the actors sauntered across the square, and from noon till dusk the Panthers brought the town to life, installing themselves either in the King of Hungary or in the Széchenyi Café.

Ijas would set off on his travels at about eight in the evening when he finally got away from the editorial office of the *Sárszeg Gazette*. He'd trudge along the side streets with his only companion, Ferenc Freund, a red-faced, jovial, sharp-witted Jewish boy who understood him, encouraged him and even dabbled a little in poetry himself. But more frequently he'd walk alone, as he did now.

In spite of their fleeting introduction at the theatre the day before, Miklós's unexpected appearance on the square set Ákos Vajkay's mind racing. There had been a time when he had sat young Ijas on his knee and pressed apricots into his mouth. But that was long ago. He hadn't mentioned it at the theatre, for the boy was sure not to remember.

At one time the Vajkays had been frequent guests in the Ijas household, at their tidy, hospitable villa in Tarliget. That was until a dark coincidence all but swept the fine and famous family off the face of the earth.

One evening János Ijas, Miklós's father, a man of considerable social standing in the county, was arrested at his villa in Tarliget by two detectives and taken away.

The case was something of a mystery. After all, his name alone served as sufficient pledge of his honour, and he was known to be a man of considerable means. And if it was true that he squandered money and sometimes risked his hand at cards, he was nevertheless respected as a thoroughly honest man. It was rumoured that the whole affair had been some kind of mistake, that he had been reported by his secret enemies and that there was no evidence against him whatsoever. He had, it was alleged, once sold a property through an intermediary who had accepted the sum of 1,500 forints from a first buyer, but then, when a second appeared, prepared to pay a higher price, had made a separate deal with him. The first buyer, who had thus lost the property he sought, reported Ijas to the authorities by way of revenge, claiming that he had never been reimbursed, and that the sale had already been officially registered.

The details remained somewhat obscure before the public, but Ijas was detained on remand and was refused bail at any sum. Whether or not the hearing ever actually took place, no one could remember. But it was a fact that poor old János Ijas was not released from jail until some eighteen months later, mentally and physically a broken man, whereupon he went abroad and died. Anguish had already driven his wife to the grave during his imprisonment.

At the time the newspapers had written this and that about the case. Especially when the tragedy of the father was followed by that of his eldest son. Jenő Ijas had been stationed in Sárszeg as a lieutenant in the Hungarian army. Because of the rumours surrounding his father's case, proceedings were taken against him too, in order to establish whether, under the circumstances, he could still be considered worthy of his commission. The lieutenant did not wait for the outcome of the investigation. One morning he walked out to the Tarliget estate and there, beneath the huge walnut tree, shot himself in the head with his service revolver. In a farewell letter he pinned to his military tunic, he wrote that this was the least he could do to defend his father's honour and good name.

Only the fifteen-year-old Miklós was left alive. He was taken in by his relations, who brought him up on the Hungarian plain. Here he rode and exercised in the open air, while doing his fair share of eating and sleeping. Later he applied to study law at the University of Kolozsvár but never sat his exams, and learned English instead. When the scandal died down in his home town, he suddenly turned up in Sárszeg, to everyone's surprise, as a journalist.

Because of his awkward situation, Miklós kept himself to himself. Even Feri Füzes picked a quarrel with him and spoke ill of him to others. The Gentlemen's Club refused to grant him membership. Thus he spent his mornings in the café behind a newspaper and his afternoons in his rented digs, writing. He was seen as something of an eccentric, an ardent devotee of the latest artistic fad, the Secession. The only reason he was out strolling now was that he carried a poem in his head. He had set out in the vain hope that it would take shape along the way, but the words spun in nebulous circles and remained worn, dull and vacant. He sauntered bareheaded in his English suit and slither of a lilac tie, a trilby in his hand. His thick chestnut hair plunged over his steep forehead, exuding eternal youth.

Glimpsing the Vajkays he looked up and hurried over towards Ákos. The day before he had found something deeply sympathetic about the old man's timid, wavering reticence. He stretched out his hand.

'Hello, Ákos.'

Vajkay shook his hand warmly, as if apologising, in everyone's name, for all that had happened.

'Hello, young man.'

Ijas faltered for a moment, then asked:

'Which way are you heading?'

'Home.'

And because he couldn't decide what else to do, and was weary of brooding over his poem, Miklós strung along with them.

'If you don't mind,' he said.

Ákos bowed, the woman lowered her gaze. Young men always made her feel awkward.

They ambled on through the mild evening air in which the houses of Sárszeg stood immobile with a certain false pathos, as if they were still waiting for something to happen.

'Have you much to do at the *Gazette*?' Ákos asked, simply making conversation.

'Enough.'

'I can well imagine. To write a newspaper every day. All those articles. In these hard times, with the world all upside down . . . that Dreyfus business . . . the strikes . . .'

'Five thousand are on strike in Brazil,' Mother ventured warily.

'Where?' asked Miklós.

'In Brazil,' Ákos repeated with conviction. 'Why, only the other day we read about it in a Budapest daily.'

'Possible,' said Ijas. 'Yes, I remember reading something,' he mumbled indifferently.

He breathed a deep sigh.

'I'm working on something else right now.'

He was thinking of his poem, which would appear in the Sunday edition of the *Gazette*, and he gave a twitch of his lips, affecting sensitivity, as he always did when alluding to his unrealised literary ambitions and seeking recognition.

But the allusion was wasted. Ákos had never read his poems. Mother might well have, but she never looked at the authors' names. She didn't think it important.

They reached the corner of Petőfi Street, which stretched deserted, deep into the silence. Miklós stopped.

'What a miserable wilderness this is,' he said. 'How can people bear to live here? If only I could get to Budapest. I was there last week . . . Ah, Budapest!'

To this he received no reply. All the same it seemed to him they had listened without ill will. And as his confidence in the elderly couple grew, he was overcome by an urge to open his heart to them.

'It was the first time I'd been to the capital,' he began, 'since my father died.'

He had mentioned his father. The one person whose name no one dared to speak and whose death had lain silenced under a cloud of shame. This drew the Vajkays closer to the boy.

'Ah, yes, poor fellow,' they said together.

'You knew him, didn't you?' said Miklós, looking at Ákos.

'I did indeed. And liked him. And respected him. He was a very dear friend.'

Their pace slackened. Ákos knitted his brow. How children suffer for their parents, and parents for their children.

Then the woman spoke.

'Our families used to meet. They came to us, we went to them. You, Miklós, were only little then, six or seven. You and Jenő would play at soldiers. We'd sit out on the veranda. By that big, long table.'

'A damn good man,' Ákos interrupted.

'I can hardly remember his face,' said Ijas gravely.

The three of them had arrived beneath a gas lamp. Ákos stopped and looked at Ijas.

'He was about your height. Yes, about as tall. You're a lot like him. But your father was more strongly built.'

'Later he lost weight. Grew terribly thin. He suffered a great deal. We all did. My mother was always in tears. My brother . . . you know. And me.'

'You were just a child.'

'Yes, and I didn't really understand it all then. But later. It was hard, my dear Ákos, very hard. They wanted me to be a lawyer. I could probably have found a position in the county administration. But the people . . . I went to Hamburg. On foot. I wanted to run away to America, where all cheats and embezzlers go.'

He laughed. This laugh offended Ákos. Was it possible that someone could speak so openly about his inner feelings, could confess almost boastfully about what hurt inside? Or maybe it no longer hurt. After all, he had laughed.

'But I didn't go to America,' Miklós continued. 'I stayed here. Just for that, I stayed here. I began

writing. But believe me, I'm more distant from any-
body now than if I had gone to America.'

How so? Ákos couldn't understand. It was just
high-flown, childish bravado. But he looked closely at
the boy and gradually noticed something about his
youthful face. It reminded him a little of Wun-Hi's,
hidden behind a mask of thick make-up. It was as if
Miklós too wore a mask, only a harder, more rigid
one, petrified by pain.

'To me it makes no difference now,' Ijas began
again, 'what Feri Füzes says, or anyone in Sárszeg, or
anywhere else.'

He seemed to mean what he said, for he spoke in a
harsh voice and strutted with steely resolve.

At any rate, they were strange fellows, these bohem-
ians. They lounged around doing nothing and told you
they were working; they were frightfully miserable
and yet would tell you that they were perfectly happy.
They had more troubles than others but seemed to
bear them better, as if they fed on suffering.

Even Zányi hadn't seemed terribly distraught at
being deserted by Olga Orosz. At the Lord Lieutenant's lunch party he had entertained the ladies with
great ease, gesticulating with a lightly bandaged hand.
Tonight he'd get made up again, and on with the
show. Szolyvay was often so short of money that he
couldn't even afford dinner and had to borrow from
Papa Fehér; even so, he showed no lack of self-esteem.
And this poor, unfortunate child, who had every
reason to complain, simply bragged, speaking of life

to one who had already lived so long, advising him, lecturing him and defying all dissent.

Such characters seemed so remote, as if they lived on an island far from the laws of all humankind. If only there were a bridge. A bridge over to this island, this security, this painted façade. But there was no bridge. One couldn't live life like a comedy or fancy-dress parade. For there were those who knew only pain; cruel, amorphous pain, and nothing else. They bury themselves within it, plunging deeper and deeper into a grief that is theirs alone, into an endless abyss, a dark and bottomless pit which finally caves in above them and traps them there for good. There is no way out.

Ákos could no longer listen to his young friend, who was now propounding all kinds of confused ideas about the eternal nature of suffering. He spoke in detail about his poems, about those he had already written and those he was yet to write, and kept repeating the words:

'Work. One has to work.'

Ákos quickly picked up on this.

'Yes, my boy, work. There's nothing nobler than work.'

Ijas stopped talking. It was quite clear that they were at cross purposes, that the couple didn't understand him. But they had listened to him all the same, and out of gratitude he turned his attention to the woman.

'Is Skylark still not back?' he asked.

Mrs Vajkay shuddered. The question was so sudden and unexpected. He was the first person to mention her in the five days she had been away. And by her nickname, too.

'No,' the woman replied, 'she's due back on Friday.'

'I can imagine how you must miss her.'

'Terribly,' said the woman. 'But she works herself to death at home. So we sent her off to the plain. To rest.'

'To rest,' said Father, mechanically echoing his wife's last words, as he often did when he was agitated and sought to silence his thoughts beneath the sound of his own voice.

Ijas noticed this. He looked into the old man's eyes, as Ákos had looked into his, and felt such pity for him that it wrung his heart. What stagnant, primal depths of pain could be disturbed by just a couple of words.

Miklós stuck to his new task and went on inquiring, probing.

The woman was glad of his attention, although she could not quite fathom its intent. She turned towards the young man.

'The two of you haven't met, have you, Miklós?'

'No, madam,' Ijas replied, 'I've not yet had the pleasure. Of course I've seen her once or twice. At a meeting of the Mary Society, for example. She seemed most enthusiastic.'

'Oh, she's awfully conscientious.'

'And with you. I've seen you all walking together. She's always in between.'

'Yes, yes.'

'She seems very kindly and . . . straightforward.'

'Bless her soul,' said the woman, raising her eyes to the heavens.

'She must be a most refined and pleasant creature. Quite different from the other girls round here.'

'If Skylark could only hear,' said Mother with a sigh, 'how pleased she'd be. And she would be ever so pleased to meet you in person. She's fond of poetry too. She has a little book, hasn't she, Father, where she copies down all those pretty poems.'

Ákos tapped the wall with his stick, for the voices he heard within him were louder than those without. He did all he could to drown them. Ijas went on talking. He asked all about Skylark, about every detail of her existence, his questions often as precise as those of Dr Gál when interviewing a patient on a house call. He was trying to draw an accurate mental portrait.

No one had ever shown such interest in their daughter, or spoken of her with such warmth and kindness.

He did not suggest that she was pretty, but neither that she was plain. He didn't lie. Instead he hovered between the two extremes and avoided the danger area altogether, shifting direction and leaving every option open. The woman fed on his every word, and in her soul a vague hope began to stir, a dim presentiment she didn't even dare to admit to herself.

'You really must visit us one day, Miklós,' she said. 'If you can spare the time, of course. Do come and see us.'

'If I may be so bold,' said Ijas.

They had reached their own house, accompanied all

the way by a young man. This didn't happen often. In fact this was the first time.

Ákos shook Ijas by the hand.

'Thank you, my dear boy,' he said, then turned inside.

The iron gate banged shut behind them.

Miklós looked through the grille into the garden. Here all was silence and solitude.

He looked at the decorative glass balls among the flowers, the stone garden gnome on the lawn, who seemed to stand on guard. A sunflower hung its head in the failing evening light, as if blindly searching for the sun on the ground. The sun into which it would usually stare and which was now nowhere to be found.

He could hear rummaging from inside the house, the old couple preparing for rest. And he could see quite clearly before him the wretched rooms, where suffering collected like unswept dust in the corners, the dust of lives in painful heaps, piled up over many long years. He shut his eyes and drank in the garden's bitter fragrance. At such times Miklós Ijas was 'working'.

He stood for some minutes before the gate with all the patience of a lover waiting for the appearance of his beloved. But he was waiting for no one. He was no lover in a worldly sense; the only love he knew was that of divine understanding, of taking a whole life into his arms, stripping it of flesh and bone, and feeling into its depths as if they were his own. From this, the greatest pain, the greatest happiness is born: the hope that we too will one day be understood, strangers will accept our words, our lives, as if they were their own.

All he had heard about his father had made him receptive to the suffering of others. Until then he had wanted nothing to do with those who lived and moved around him – with Környey, the drunken Szunyogh, Szolyvay the ham actor, and Doba, who was always silent. Not even with Skylark. For yes, at first sight they had seemed worthless, twisted and distorted, their souls curling hideously inwards. They had no tragedy, for how could tragedy begin to grow in such a wasteland? Yet how profound, how human they all were. How much like him. Once this became clear it could never be forgotten. So he did have something in common with them, after all.

He took this lesson with him. His steps were firmer, surer, as he strode back down Petőfi Street. The poem he had been carrying inside his head had been a bad poem and he gave it no further thought. He'd write about other things, perhaps about these people and all they had told him. About the veranda and that long, long table where they once had sat, and sat no more.

At Széchenyi Square he broke into a run. He hurried down Gombkötő Street, for here, next to the bakery, lived Kladek, the senior editor and publisher of the *Sárszeg Gazette*.

This bearded, slow-witted, but cultivated and conscientious old man no longer even visited the editorial office, and only demanded of his assistant editor that he call on him once a day. He sat beside a paraffin lamp in his ravaged room where books lay strewn about the floor and the windows were all but barricaded by discarded newspapers piled six feet high. He had lost his grip on this cursed modern age and no longer cared what the next generation made of it, no longer cared, however much young Ijas praised the Secession in his paper.

He rummaged in his pocket for a leader Feri Füzes had written about the effect of hoarfrost on grapes. He gave this to Ijas and told him to take it to the printers, to give the peasants of Sárszeg something to read about.

All that remained for Ijas now was to take a call from Pest about the Dreyfus trial and the latest political events. He had to hurry, because the telephone usually rang at nine.

VIII

---

in which is contained the full text of Skylark's letter

Ákos was just about to set out from home the following afternoon when he met the postman at the gate. A registered letter had arrived.

Skylark. He immediately recognised the pointed, spidery lettering which reminded him of gothic script and also of his mother's hand.

He opened the letter there in the street. At any other time he'd have used his penknife for this purpose, for he believed in order in all matters, however small. But now he ripped the envelope open with his fingers, and with such excitement that he tore the letter too, both in the middle and on one side. He had to piece the fragments back together.

Oblivious to the passers-by, who bumped into him and stared after him as he went, he eagerly read the letter syllable by syllable. The words marched across the page in exemplary, solid lines. The writing was clear, but on this occasion Skylark had used a pencil, a particularly hard pencil that scored the paper with faint, unshaded lines like scratches made by a needle. By the time Ákos had fully deciphered the text, he had reached the park.

Here he put the letter into his pocket and walked on with his hands behind his back. Afternoon strollers lingered in the bare and withered park, where only a handful of hawthorn and rosebushes still managed to survive. The lawn was parched yellow from the heat, strewn with rubbish and scattered sheets of newspaper. Ákos sat down on a bench and spread the letter over his knees.

Skylark's spelling was impeccable and she wrote in the clear, orderly Hungarian she had been taught at the Ladies' College. Her style, however, was a little wooden. As soon as she took a pen in her hand, her mode of expression changed and she fell under the spell of textbook composition. At such times she could always see her former teacher, the strict Mrs Janecz, standing before her in a starched white collar and black tie. She became so terrified of making mistakes that she chose words she'd never dream of using in everyday conversation.

Her writing lost any appearance of naturalness and took on a tone more elevated and enthusiastic than she intended.

Ákos reread the long letter in which his daughter gave a detailed account of all that had happened so far. Thus:

Tarkő Plain 4 September 1899
Monday evening, half past six o'clock
My dear, sweet parents,
Forgive me for not having written to you earlier,

but I have until this moment been so very busy with all the many joys of life in the plains, and my hospitable relations have provided so very much for my entertainment, that it is only now I have been able to find time for correspondence.

I have been searching for a pen for days.

Yesterday I found the only one in the house on Uncle Béla's desk, but even this was rusty and the inkwell had, in the great heat, run completely dry. Cousin Berci at last placed this pencil at my disposal. Thus I am forced to write in pencil. For this too I beg your forgiveness.

I shall begin at the beginning.

The journey was most agreeable. As the train departed and you, my dear parents, disappeared before my eyes, I entered my compartment in which my two polite travelling companions already sat, a young man and an aged Roman Catholic priest. I was at once absorbed by the passing landscape, the pleasing variety and fresh colours of which claimed my full attention. I observed the beauties of nature, which only began to unfold in all their true splendour beyond the boundaries of our town, addressing my very spirit with peaceful, consoling words. With nature I conversed for the entire duration of my journey.

I reflected on the past, my thoughts devoted, above all, to you. Time flew by and I arrived punctually. They awaited me with a carriage. In the evening I enjoyed an appetising supper and convivial conversation in the circle of my relations.

I received a hearty welcome from all – Uncle Béla, Aunt Etelka and Cousin Berci.

Only Tiger seemed to take no pleasure in my arrival.

This good and faithful dog did not recognise me and went on barking, snarling and growling for some time. I didn't even dare venture outside alone for several days. Then this morning on the veranda, I finally succeeded in placating her. I dipped my plain-cake in the milk and gave it to her. Now we are the best of friends.

It is seven years since my last visit, in which time much has changed. Can you imagine, there is now a garden on the hill, with tropical plants and rhododendrons? There is also a winding path leading down to the brook, from which they have cleared away all the bulrushes and on which one may even row a boat. Only in spring, of course, for now it is quite dry. In a word, the place is quite divine.

Berci, whom I had not seen since he visited us in Sárszeg when he was eleven, has just matriculated from a private establishment in Budapest. He passed his examinations, with some difficulty I am told, and will now study at the School of Agriculture in Magyaróvár.

I find Uncle Béla a little changed. His hair is hoary at the temples, and I had somehow expected him to look different. It was hard to get used to him at first and I kept looking at him with a smile. He would look back at me, also with a smile. 'Have I grown old?' he asked. 'No,' I replied, 'not in the least.' At this everyone began to laugh, including Uncle Béla.

Aunt Etelka scolds him continually for his smoking, but it seems as if she'll never persuade him to give the habit up. But he doesn't eat supper any more, and only has a cup of milk in the evening, without sugar, and a slice of aleuron-bread, which he always offers me, in fun of course.

I'm still his little favourite. He sits me down next to him, kisses and cuddles me and says what he always used to say to me when I was a little girl, 'Never fear, Skylark dear, good old Uncle Béla's here.' At this we both giggle.

All through supper they ask me to talk about you. They were most amused by how worried you were about me. 'A bad penny . . .' said Uncle Béla, with that sweet humour of his.

We chatted until almost midnight, when they showed me to the spare room. I soon fell asleep in the nice, soft bed.

I awoke at dawn to an infernal racket. I could hear shrieking out on the veranda. Guests had arrived from Budapest, the Thurzó girls, whom they had invited long before, but who had never turned up. At breakfast they introduced themselves and asked if I'd allow their four large suitcases to be taken into the spare room. I gladly granted them their request. They spent the whole morning there unpacking. As I prefer to be alone, I recommended that they stay in the spare room, while I moved in with Aunt Etelka for a few days.

Since then I've been sleeping on the divan, beside Aunt Etelka, but it's much more pleasant this way. I could never really become friendly with these girls. Zelma, the eldest, is such a little secessionist! She smokes cigarettes and doesn't wear a corset. She changes costume three times a day, once for lunch, once for dinner and once again for tennis. She laughs at me because I bring home a large bunch of wild flowers every day.

She finds wild flowers ugly. She likes only camellias and orchids.

Berci would appear to be courting the younger sister. She's still only a little girl, sixteen years old. They hide away together in the house, then steal out in the morning, running off unchaperoned into the forest, returning awfully late.

Yesterday Aunt Etelka asked me to go with them, but I shan't accept that role any more. What children! It would seem that they're actually quite serious. Uncle Béla teases them cruelly at table. Berci goes quite red, but Klári doesn't.

The following day another guest arrived, Feri Olcsvay, who, I fancy, may have taken an interest in Zelma. He at least is an attentive and courteous young man. He spent a long time talking to me. We even worked out that we are very distantly related. I looked at his signet ring and from the lily surmised that we belong to the same original family – the Boksas, isn't it? He maintains, however, that the background on their coat of arms is not scarlet like ours, but gold, whereas the lily isn't gold, but scarlet. In any case, it's not sure whether he descends from the Olcsvays of Kisvárad or Nagyvárad. No one has ever been able to shed any clear light on this. His father believes they descended from the Kisvárad branch, but in the National Museum they told him he probably came from the Nagyvárad Olcsvays. Poor boy, now he really doesn't know where he stands at all. I told him to turn to Father, who'd be able to decide the matter at once. Feri promised to look Father up when he's next in Sárszeg.

Otherwise we're having a splendid time. It is quite enchanting to wake to the sounds of the plain, to the dreamy tinkle of cowbells and the cooing of turtle doves. And those darling yellow chicks who hide away cheeping under the wings of the brooding hens. How sweet life is in the country! How delightful their work must be! They're preparing for the harvest and have already brought the barrels out of the cellar. Uncle Béla is busy fumigating them stave by stave. The crop promises to be good, and they say there'll be an excellent festival.

Now I shall describe how I spend my days here. I rise early, at six, to watch the glorious sunrise, then go for a little walk with Aunt Etelka before helping her with the housework. In the kitchen she calls me her right hand. In the afternoon I go to the apiary with Józsi, the young gardener. I simply can't stop marvelling at the industry of those busy bees. Józsi can't believe how brave I am – for a girl, that is. Of course the Thurzó girls scream if a bee flies anywhere near them.

You know I cannot bear to be idle. I'm still crocheting the yellow tablecloth and should have finished it in a day or two. But it gets dark here rather early.

At about six in the evening, when they light the lamps, I take up Jókai's *The Baron's Sons*, which I've read before, but whose real beauty I have only now come to appreciate. Ödön Baradlay moves me to tears, while Zebulon Tallérossy makes me laugh out loud. How well our great storyteller knew the secrets of the heart and how ornately he expressed them! Unfortunately I've only been able to find Volume II. The first volume seems to have gone astray.

Tonight there is a ball in Tarkő, and the Thurzó girls, Berci and Feri Olcsvay have driven over there in two carriages, together with Aunt Etelka. They begged me to go with them, but I declined. I said I had nothing suitable to wear. I really shouldn't enjoy myself without you, and, to be honest, I didn't find the prospect of an evening with the Thurzó girls especially alluring either. And anyway, last night, at about one o'clock, my tooth (the one I last had filled) started aching so much that I had to wake up Aunt Etelka. Don't worry, it didn't hurt for long, because I rubbed my gums with rum and the pain died down. But I was afraid it might flare up again, so I stayed at home, holding the fort with Uncle

Béla. He's already gone to bed now, and I'm sitting in my cosy little room, writing to you.

But what a selfish thing I am! I ramble on about myself, bragging and complaining, and have completely forgotten about you, all on your own. Is Father very busy? Is he working on another family tree? Is Mother, poor dear, growing weary of all the housework? Is the food at the restaurant absolutely ghastly? Are you in good health? Are you missing your naughty, ungrateful daughter just a tiny bit? Did you find the pantry key, which, at the last minute, I left under the blue tablecloth?

I'm with you in my every thought, and sometimes when I laugh here, I suddenly grow sad, because I see the two of you sitting in the dining room alone, my poor, dear parents. I'm actually quite ready to come home. They're trying dreadfully hard to make me stay another week, but however nice a little more holiday would be, I wouldn't stay for all the tea in China. I shall be home, as promised, on Friday evening with the half-past-eight (20.25) train. I can hardly wait to embrace you both again.

I must hurry to conclude these lines. I want to send them off tonight with the coachman who'll drive out to Tarkő after midnight for the girls. A hundred kisses and embraces from your loving daughter

Skylark

That was all. There the letter came to an end.

Ákos sighed. He carefully slipped his spectacles back into their paper case.

The letter still lay open on his knees.

A single name kept coming to his mind. He muttered it to himself under his breath:

'Olga Orosz.'

And it wasn't the Tarkő plain he saw before him in his mind's eye, nor the divan on which his daughter slept, nor the Thurzó girls, but, even more clearly than on stage two days before, he saw Olga Orosz, kissing Sir Reginald Fairfax on the mouth.

She wouldn't understand this letter. Nor would she understand why its every word cut him to the quick, why its every observation was so special – that a path now wound its way down from the hill, that the rhododendrons were in bloom, that they already lit the lamps at six, and were preparing for the harvest. Olga Orosz would laugh at all this with her husky, throaty trill.

The children, the little cops and robbers who had till then been playing in the park, were now gone. Dusk was falling. In the country, after sunset, every child belongs at home.

Now common soldiers strolled through the park, gently swinging the calloused hands of their housemaid sweethearts – hands that fitted snugly in their own thick palms. From this coarseness something sweet might yet be born. Little parlour maids, buxom cooks and sluttish Soldier-Suzies in grubby dresses came arm in arm with these rough peasant lads who'd curse in the barracks, be clouted and clapped in irons

by their sergeants, but now ambled along quite harm-
lessly.

Their blue eyes were glazed with dumb delight,
caring about nothing, no one. Their boyish faces and
pug noses red with schnapps, they looked like lost
orphans, wandering dreamily through some enchanted
garden of love, the women leading them onwards.
Every now and then the couples stopped and gazed
deep into one another's eyes. They sat down on
wooden benches near the bushes, waiting for it to
grow completely dark.

How squalid it all was, here and at the theatre too,
among the shabby props and decorations. There was
no justice in the world, no justice anywhere. Everything was meaningless. Nothing mattered at all.

Ákos reeled with hatred, staring at the couples with
an open mouth. He was startled by a light touch on his
hand.

'So here you are.'

His wife had been looking for him. They had
arranged to meet in the park before going to dinner.

'What happened?' she asked after Ákos had risen to
his feet and they had walked about ten paces.

'Nothing,' said the man. 'That is, Skylark's
written.'

'Where's the letter?'

'Here,' said Ákos, reaching into his pocket.

But he couldn't find the letter. Neither in one
pocket, nor in the other.

They hurried back to the bench.

But it wasn't there either.

The letter had disappeared somewhere, fallen to the ground, perhaps, and been whisked away by the wind, along with all the torn newspaper sheets and other rubbish.

Ákos tried to suppress his irritation.

'What did she say?' asked his wife.

'She's fine. Having a wonderful time.'

'And her health?'

'She's perfectly well. Only a slight toothache.'

'Poor thing.'

'But she rubbed rum on it,' said Ákos. 'Good, strong rum, and it went away.'

This comforted the woman.

They dined with Környey, and not in the worst of spirits. They stayed until eleven o'clock. Because the roast pork and red cabbage were rather greasy, Ákos took the exceptional liberty of allowing himself half a bottle of wine.

IX

-----

in which is comprised a description of the shindig, the Panthers' famous weekly revelry

A nd as for Thursday . . . Well, Thursday was simply Thursday.

A Thursday was no ordinary day. It was not marked with red letters in the calendar, but in Sárszeg it was no less notable than a Sunday. For Thursday was the day of the shindig.

The Panthers held their shindig in the clubhouse. It was the one day of the week when they could be truly alone, free of any trace of influence of womankind. The women of Sárszeg looked forward to these Thursdays with trepidation. Their husbands would stumble home at dawn, or later still, and all day long they'd be surly, red-eyed and thoroughly sick.

Ákos recalled these Thursday evenings with disgust, and when, the day before, Környey had ceremoniously invited him to join the Panthers at the club, he had racked his brains for excuses. Poppycock, insisted Környey, unmoved. Ákos explained that, unfortu-

nately, he and his wife were already expected somewhere else. Not good enough, came the reply. And
thus it went on until Ákos had finally promised to
make an appearance early in the afternoon. Just for a
few minutes, mind, a quarter of an hour at the most. A
quarter of an hour and no more. He'd shake on it?
Ákos extended his hand, out of weakness, rather than
resolution, and gave his word of honour. Now there
could be no turning back.

In the afternoon he allowed himself a prudent hour's
sleep and woke refreshed. Wearing dove-grey gloves
and carrying a silver-pommelled cane, he stepped into
the foyer of the clubhouse, opened the huge glass door
and climbed the steps to the first floor.

In the hall he met an old acquaintance, Básta, the
liveried attendant, on his way to the library with two
large china bowls in whose vinegary water sprigs of
lettuce swam, and slices of hard-boiled egg. He set
them down on an empty bookshelf – where the food
always stood on Thursday evenings – and, clicking his
heels before the honourable gentleman, relieved Ákos
of his cane and led him inside.

The courtesy was superfluous, for Ákos knew his
way around. Nothing had changed at all since his last
visit.

In the reading room – as of old – sat the solitary
figure of Sárcsevits, a rich, laconic bachelor of independent means, who now, as ever, was reading *Le
Figaro*. He always read *Le Figaro*, and thus was generally held to be a cultivated European.

To the left stood the more spacious drawing room, furnished with leather couches.

The Panthers could already be heard deep in conversation.

Ákos made his way towards them.

When he first opened the drawing-room door he couldn't see a thing. Clouds of smoke billowed up before him, which even the gas lamps burning on the walls and ceiling were unable to disperse. These clouds forewarned of the approaching storm.

Some thirty or forty figures slowly emerged from the general haze. For a moment Ákos stood bewildered.

Then they spotted him, and he was greeted with cheers of jubilation. The Panthers, those moustachioed wild beasts of revelry, leaped from their seats, sprang towards him and spun him to and fro among them.

'Ákos,' they cried from all corners. 'Good old Ákos! Come in, come in and join us.'

Total strangers introduced themselves, younger men who immediately addressed him in the familiar form.

'*Servus humillimus*, pleased to meet you, where have you been hiding all these years?'

There were also those who scolded him:

'You've a lot to answer for, old man. But you'll make up for it tonight.'

The voice of Környey, however, rang out above all others:

'Forgive ye the repentant sinner!'

Roars of laughter pealed throughout the Panthers' den.

Környey stood two heads taller than his comrades in a gold-piped, cornflower-blue military tunic.

He crushed the brittle bones of Ákos's narrow hand in his iron clasp, famed for twisting silver forint coins, and, as head Panther, welcomed him with a certain stiff and formal conviviality. There was something austere, almost frightening about him.

He did not tarry long with Ákos. For on Thursdays Környey had to dash to and fro, welcoming new arrivals and discussing urgent culinary matters with the staff. Even now he was called away to the library to inspect the salad. He had more to do on such occasions than at the time of the great steam-mill fire.

All in all, Ákos's appearance had created quite a stir.

Priboczay embraced him, pressing the old man's face to his own and refusing to let go. Finally he planted a tender, masculine kiss on Ákos's cheek.

The chemist was in tears. His eyes were as weak as his heart, and whenever he met an old friend they melted, like hair in a fire, from the sheer warmth that coursed through his whole being.

He rummaged for his handkerchief.

When he had dried his tears, he took Ákos by both hands and held him beneath the chandelier to examine him more thoroughly.

'My dear old fellow,' he said in astonishment, 'you look so much younger.'

'Nonsense.'

'So help me, it's true,' he insisted. 'You're in excellent colour.'

All who stood around them mumbled in agreement.

Ákos's face had indeed filled out from his afternoon nap, the skin exuding a rosy, priestly glow. His forehead also wore a tint of red, as did the two loose bags of skin beneath his eyes.

'By Jove,' said Priboczay, 'you've turned into a proper cavalier.' And he looked down at Ákos's dove-grey gloves.

These Ákos removed at once.

'And how tall you stand,' Priboczay continued. 'None of that stooping any more. *Canis Mater*! What have you been taking? What have you done?'

'I've been to the barber's,' stuttered Ákos. 'Maybe that's it.'

'No, no, you've grown younger. Ten years younger. Five at the very least. The quiet life, eh?'

A thin, sly smile hid in Ákos's moustache, where the Tiszaújlak wax still held firm. He didn't know where to look.

'I'm old, my friend,' he said at last, 'an old fossil just like you, like all of you.' And he hung his head in mock self-pity.

Priboczay took him by the arm and led him round the room, introducing him to those smaller groups of Panthers who already sat sipping their drinks in the background or gossiping in the window bays.

And yes, they had indeed grown old. Some of the Panthers had gold teeth; most wore dentures or gum plates. Gone were the thick black curls he used to see on Thursday evenings; and what was left of them was covered with rime. Only the moustaches were haunted here and there by the odd, spectral brown hair. Some of them had grown completely bald, their bare skulls round and shiny like ivory billiard balls, or pointed like eggs.

The tables, however, remained unchanged: the black marble tables crowded with battalions of slender wine bottles and mouldy water carafes. And the green baize card tables with their inlaid copper ashtrays.

And the large painting on the wall. Count István Széchenyi.

He had not grown old.

Left hand on his hip, near his sword belt, pushing open his short, fur-lined coat, he stood as of old, his domed forehead surrounded by tousled, floating curls, his restless eyes burning with character, vigour and intelligence as they looked down upon what had become of his noble ideas, the debating circles and clubs he had founded to promote the refinement of polite society and social intercourse. But in the thick smoke, which one could have cut with a knife, even Count István Széchenyi cannot have seen too well.

Básta, the attendant, stopped in front of Ákos, wearing a blue and white ceremonial uniform and a waxed moustache whose ends narrowed into an almost invisibly thin thread way out beyond his cheeks. He was holding a large wine tray and had a napkin over his arm. Standing to attention, he poured the gentlemen some wine.

Priboczay raised his glass.

'Welcome!'

He downed his wine in one, as was right and proper on such occasions.

'Your health!'

'Your health!'

They shook hands and sat down on a sofa.

A quarter of an hour later Ákos made ready to leave.

'Now I really should be getting along.'

'You'll do nothing of the sort, dear boy.'

Környey, the perfect host, possessed an innate ability to appear at the slightest hint of danger, whenever someone was contemplating escape.

'Out of the question,' he thundered. 'You're staying right where you are.' And he clasped the old man in his steely arms.

He led Ákos away to the smokiest corner of the room, where, beneath a hanging lamp, four men sat playing taroc.

'I've brought you a fifth hand,' said Környey to the players.

Taroc was Ákos's great weakness, but also his great strength.

No one played with greater skill, ingenuity and passion. So profound was his knowledge of the game that he was considered something of an authority and had often been asked to adjudicate in controversial situations, as the final court of appeal.

'*A la russe*?' asked Ákos casually.

'That's right,' came the answer from the table as Galló, the amenable lawyer, himself a renowned master of the game, raised his wise head from the smoke of his own cigar.

He rose to his feet.

'I'm just about to deal.'

Two other players had risen with him, Doba and a squat man in a raw silk suit. This was István Kárász, father of Dani Kárász and owner of a thousand acres, whose shaven head was burnt jet black from the sun. Only the fourth player remained seated: László Ladányi, parliamentary delegate for the Royal Town of Sárszeg during the 1848 revolution. With his grizzled, tight-clipped beard and bushy eyebrows he reminded one of the poet Miklós Zrinyi.

Relations between Ladányi and Ákos had been strained for many years.

The delegate – known to all and sundry as 'the old ranter' – was one of those passionate exaggerators of the extreme left who, in confidential conversation, made no secret of their undying commitment to the resolutions of the Debrecen Parliament of 1849, and of their perpetual readiness to contribute to the downfall of the House of Habsburg in payment for the crimes it had committed against the Hungarian nation. In 1849 his grandfather had been hanged from a pear tree by imperial soldiers. He would often mention this when canvassers appeared at his door with flags and torches, and he blasted them with a voice broken for good from swallowing all the nation's bitterness. He knew Ákos well, as a timid fellow who always voted for the government candidate, even though, deep down, he may himself have leaned towards the stalwart forty-eighters. But he lacked the stomach for a fight, and sought instead to remain at peace with himself, his family and friends, and therefore favoured compromise, all forms of compromise, including the Compromise of 1867.

Ladányi had been known, on occasion, to speak harshly of the man.

But now, with Ákos standing directly above him, and the others urging him to join them on their feet, he finally stood up. Hungarians fight by the sword and make peace by the glass. He offered Ákos his hand.

'Join us,' he said in his grating voice.

It was an opportunity not to be missed. The taroc players fêted Ákos like some celebrity from distant climes. The large, special, grey-backed taroc cards tempted him too. It was all too much to resist. Ákos finally surrendered.

'To hell with it!'

Reassured, Környey withdrew.

Ákos settled down at the table, on whose marble top the odd drop of wine sparkled, spilled from the bottle at pouring. Also on the table lay neat black slates with the names of the players written with sticks of carefully sharpened chalk.

Galló dealt.

Ákos took the nine cards in his hands, his practised fingers ordering them with lightning speed, greeting the images which spoke of ancient worlds and happy times: the juggler with his human-headed lyre and sword, the hoop-skirted Spanish lady with her castanets, the top trump in gaudy clown's garb and a two-headed hat, the giant twenty-one, the squatting Turk with his long-stemmed pipe, the honours who beat all other cards, hence their name. A delightful, familiar crew. Lovers embracing by a wall, an ancient soldier bidding his sweetheart farewell, a ship setting out across the seas. A splendid hand indeed.

The players inspected their cards, then looked at each other no less intently. They blinked cunningly, for their faces were as important as their cards. What were they scheming, what tricks had they in store, what traps and machinations were being prepared?

'Pass,' said Ákos.

'Pass,' said Kárász, who sat beside him.

Ákos took great pleasure in his meditations. He even lit a cigar to oil the machinery of his mind.

Taroc is not one of those upstart, good-for-nothing games they dream up nowadays. Its roots reach way back into the past, and it boasts the noblest of ancestors. It stems from Asia, like our heroic forebears, and demands a meandering, eastern frame of mind, along with concentration, imagination and perpetual presence of spirit. It is like a wily tale with a crafty introduction, an intriguing exposition and a surprisingly sudden denouement. It demands much racking of brains, but is not intellectually dry. It is a thoroughly enjoyable game which took the work of several generations to chisel into its present, ingenious form.

Kárász drew a three from the pack.

'I call twenty,' he said.

Doba and Ladányi passed again.

Ákos twirled his moustache.

'Double,' he announced merrily.

The others ruminated.

Ákos and Ladányi, gradually warming to each other, played as a pair, while Doba assisted Kárász, who sat facing Ákos. They glared at one another.

Judge Doba was surprised at just how alert the old man was.

Ákos took a long, hard look at the judge. He sat in silence, just as he had sat at the theatre beside his flirtatious wife, who wore her hair like Olga Orosz and numbered even the penniless Szolyvay among her lovers – at least so Szolyvay said. Did the poor, likable judge know this? Did he at least suspect? He never spoke of it. Even now his face reflected nothing but a certain weary indifference.

He answered Ákos's double with:

'Redouble. *Tous les trois.*'

'Aha,' said Ákos to himself, '*tous les trois, tous les trois.*'

On this he pondered, which was, perhaps, his great mistake.

He, the seasoned matador, had not paid sufficient attention to the run of the cards, and by now there was nothing for it – the game had reached a fateful turn with Doba and Kárász gaining the upper hand.

Those who stood around them watching were amazed.

'Impossible!'

'This calls for a drink,' said Kárász.

Werner, the Austrian lieutenant rifleman, who had been sitting beside Ákos in total silence, poured the wine. He and his battalion had been based in Sárszeg now for some four years, but he still couldn't speak a word of Hungarian. And German he could speak only when he was sober. At times like these, however, when he'd been drinking, his German deserted him. Even his mother tongue, Moravian, refused to come to his aid. He was an excellent Panther, all the same, and was having a splendid time. He continually grinned and drank and poured.

'Not drinking?' said Ladányi to Ákos. 'It's only a light Szilványi,' he added, emptying his glass.

The words 'light Szilványi' sounded so delicious that Ákos couldn't resist.

Ladányi embraced him.

'That's my Ákos,' he said. 'Only would you mind doing me one small favour? Get rid of those damned sunflowers from your garden.'

'Whatever for?'

'They're black and yellow, old man. Can't stand the sight of those Schwarzgelb colours, not even in flowers.'

To this they filled their glasses once more.

Ákos not only knocked back the light Szilványi, but also all the other wines they set before him, the light wines from grapes grown in sandy soil and the heavy mountain wines

He totted up the scores with his chalk.

'So, how do we stand? Double, redouble, four points; *tous les trois*, two; four kings, one. Seven points all in all. That's seven kreuzers. Here you are.'

He paid, and wiped his slate with the little yellow sponge provided.

He lit a new cigar and even removed his spectacles. This was always a sure sign of his good spirits.

By now he was no different from the others. He could no longer see the party from the outside as he had on first entering the room. He didn't even notice the suffocating smell of smoke. He seemed entirely at ease, as if he had merely slept throughout his long years of absence and was now carrying on where he had left off. A brittle crust seemed to crumble and flake from his person, the top of his head began to sweat and his snowy hair seemed to melt on top of it. In his eyes, too, happy tears glistened. His ears glowed red, as old friendships revived and blossomed.

But now it was back to business, to the new game, and revenge. Ákos braced himself as the cards were being dealt, unfastening his shirt cuffs and drawing together all his strength. Then he threw himself at his adversaries with all his old confidence.

'Out with the eighteen!' he cried at once.

Where could it be, the coveted, happy eighteen? Who on earth could have it? For the moment, however, Ákos continued playing his hand.

Winking cunningly at the other players, he threw his remaining trumps on the table before them: ace, twenty-one, nineteen, and finally, after a calculated pause, he produced the missing eighteen himself.

'Ha!' the others shouted. 'He had it!'

'He called his own hand!' they chuckled, unable to believe their eyes.

'He's impossible. The old Ákos, the one and only.' They embraced him one after the other. 'You've got the devil in you, old boy,' they roared. 'This calls for a drink.' And the thunder of their laughter shook the window panes.

One game spilled into another, with Ákos shrewdly holding his own, uncovering every plot and scheme, averting every ambush. It was a long, long game.

But not for Ákos or the other players. What did they know of time, since falling captive to the magic of the cards? For all card players enjoy the intoxication of complete forgetting, and enter a separate universe whose very contours are defined by the cards.

'Vole, bull, juggler.' Ákos's words flew through the smoky air. 'Juggler, joker, final trick.' His opponents hissed and gasped in disbelief.

Ákos gave them all a thorough thrashing. Only then did he glance at the clock ticking away on the wall before him. It was already after half past nine. He was suddenly seized by an inexplicable melancholy.

For a moment he hung his head, crestfallen after his unaccustomed frivolity. He stared straight through his companions as if they were not there at all.

The waiters announced that dinner would be served.

They made their way into the library, where dinner was taken on Thursday evenings.

Sárcsevits had still not finished *Le Figaro*. He sat to one side, beneath an electric light by the wall, and went on studying every word. The others planted themselves down at the table, which was decorated with flowers.

It was a doughty Hungarian dinner: chicken stew, pasta with curd and bacon, noodles with ground poppy seed and walnut, and mouldy, smelly cheeses to follow, which went superbly with the mildly tart and musty wine.

The table was crammed full. They must have been fifty in all, for new guests had arrived for dinner. Máté Gaszner, assessor to the orphan's court, a lame and rather objectionable little man, who was popular all the same and was addressed as 'my dear Mátéka' by everyone present. Kostyál, a retired teacher from the neighbouring town who was, as they said, a 'regular trencherman'. Vereczkey, the Lord Lieutenant's private secretary, who had served in the Tyrol and knew a string of fine Italian songs. And of course Feri Füzes also put in an appearance, showing off his stupid smile, which he seemed to have polished specially for the occasion. Throughout dinner he kept repeating:

'I do adore society. I really am the most jolly of fellows.'

And Olivér Hartyányi came too, the 'atheist'.

Poor Olivér had been suffering from degenerative syphilis for years. And that, by and large, was why poor Olivér was an atheist. Towards evening he'd have himself wheeled to the club, where two attendants carried him upstairs in the large cushioned chair in which he sat in his courtyard at home. His legs were covered with a thick, woollen blanket.

He appeared particularly lively this evening, having taken a larger than usual injection of morphine before setting out. His eyes gleamed and his dilated pupils sparkled, lending a certain sharpness to his haggard, olive-green face. His eyebrows curled like caterpillars as he spoke.

He ended up beside Feri Füzes. The two men loathed each other, but loved to argue all the same, and did so endlessly.

Feri Füzes insisted on the existence of God. Olivér Hartyányi disagreed. The debate had rambled on for years, without either participant surrendering an inch of ground. Now they once more rehearsed their familiar arguments in the name of idealism and materialism. Feri Füzes curled his lips sarcastically at the mention of Darwin, not because he didn't consider the fellow a gentleman, but because he held the same opinion of Darwin as of Lajos Kossuth. Darwin had his good and bad points like anyone else. Then it was time for Olivér to play his trump card. With bitter, derisive words he painted a picture of ubiquitous ruin and decay, the only things he believed in, complete and utter destruction, the rotting human body, teeming with grubs and maggots. He spoke out loud, the more to outrage his companions at table. But they paid not the slightest notice either to him or to Feri Füzes. They were equally weary of them both.

Besides, the Gypsies had already struck up. The famous János Csinos Band stood in position by the tall folding doors and the leader, an old friend of all present, was scraping and flourishing with all his soul. He never played more sweetly than on Thursday evenings. He turned devotedly – although still keeping a respectful distance – towards István Kárász, looking up at him now and then with a dreamy smile in which many shared memories seemed to slumber. He had played at Kárász's wedding and had fiddled many a thousand-forint banknote from the landowner's pocket. Kárász would invite him to his estate once a year. The previous year he had strung a whole ham around each Gypsy's neck and made them play on thus equipped till dawn.

István Kárász, who sat between Ákos and Ladányi, stopped eating. As soon as he heard the strains of the violin he sat back in his chair, hung his arms by his sides and, with a vein beginning to bulge on his forehead, listened with mooning eyes. He appeared to remain indifferent, but gave his heart entirely to the Gypsy: to nurse it, caress it and mine its very depths. He surrendered his soul with a certain leisurely, gentlemanly nonchalance, as others might offer their feet to the pedicurist. He had more faith in the Gypsy than in his doctor, Dr Gál.

The leader, for his part, left no heartstring unplucked. He stabbed and stung, tweaked and tormented, faithful servant that he was. Soon a fat teardrop swelled in the landowner's eye and rolled its way down his sunburnt cheek. Why did Kárász cry? All of Sárszeg belonged to him. He could no longer even count his stud horses, his herds of pigs and cattle. His children and grandchildren all prospered. Who could tell what ancient memories of wedding feasts and long-abandoned reveries the music stirred within him?

Galló glared stonily into space, as if still squinting at the accused in court, refusing to be moved, repelling every last appeal to sentiment. Doba was undoubtedly thinking of his wife, wandering, God knows where, in the night. He had sunk so deep into sorrow and self-torment that he himself seemed to take fright and, as if coming up from the depths for air, drew a deep breath. Ladányi was looking directly towards Vienna, on his face the patriotic grief of four hundred years of ser-vility to the House of Habsburg. Priboczay melted, his eyes becoming two melancholy pools of tears. Feri Füzes crooned, Olivér Hartyányi growled, Szunyogh hung his heavy, drunken head, swinging it slowly to and fro like an elephant. Környey waxed bellicose; Mályvády, Sárszeg's great patron of the natural sciences, grew facetious; Kostyál became cantanker-ous; while Máté Gaszner seemed to have completely lost his mind.

Even Básta, the attendant, had finally forgotten all decorum and, no longer standing to attention – he was, after all, himself a genuine Szekler Magyar – min-gled like a brother with the other gentlemen. The wait-ers passed on tiptoe. They could sense that something extraordinary was happening here which it would be ungodly to disturb.

Sárcsevits had finished reading *Le Figaro*, right down to the last letter of the smallest classified adver-tisement. He gazed at the revellers and shook his head. He felt nothing at all. Only that it seemed a shame to waste so much time and energy. What improvidence, what nabobish profligacy, to squander all our experi-ences, to spill them carelessly, along with all the wine, on to the floor! Somewhere on the banks of the Seine, from so many good intentions, from so many colours and emotions, whole buildings could be erected, whole books could be penned. If the good gentlemen would only say what was going on in their minds at such times, more books could be written than the entire collection of the Sárszeg clubhouse library, which no one read anyway, apart from him and prosecutor Galló, and perhaps poor Olivér too, who desired, before finally climbing into his grave, to know a thing or two about this pitiful world.

But the others had no time for such things.

The leader of the Gypsy band began to play 'May Beetle'. Ákos raised his hand and stopped him. This was Ákos's song.

He called the Gypsy over and made him place a mute on the bridge of his violin. When the leader struck up again, Ákos launched into the song. At first his voice wavered a little, but soon it grew more confident, distinguished, almost arrogant. A restrained but pleasant tenor voice. Ákos drew a languid arch with his forefinger as he raised it slowly to his temple.

May beetle, may beetle, softly you hum,
I shall not ask you when summer will come . . .

Sárcsevits stood up. With a smile he turned to Feri Füzes who stood beside him.

'Is that old Vajkay?'

'The very same.'

'I'd heard he was a surly old troglodyte.'

'Not at all,' replied Feri Füzes stiffly. 'He's a most jolly and sociable fellow.'

While the gentlemen were at dinner, the drawing room was swept and aired. By the time they returned, a neat and tidy room awaited them. The warm atmosphere had disappeared with the smoke and a cold severity could be felt in the air.

In such conditions it was no longer possible simply to pick up where they had left off that afternoon. Wine was replaced by schnapps; taroc and trumps by poker and pontoon. The fun and games were over. Now came the time of the serious drinkers who stood for no frivolity, and the serious card players who no longer merely toyed with fortune, but played to raze the opposition to the ground.

Ákos found himself at a pontoon table where the stakes were five forints and they drank Kantusovszka and other Polish brandies. Környey made it his business to see that everyone drank his share.

Ákos proved himself more than equal to the task.

And he was lucky at pontoon, too.

'Nine,' he kept calling.

The crumpled banknotes lay in heaps before him, beside great piles of coppers and columns of nickel and silver coins. Soon the steel-blue one-thousand notes began appearing from leather wallets. Ákos simply couldn't get rid of his money.

'Eight,' his partners called.

'Nine,' Ákos replied.

Ákos both fretted and laughed at the same time. Out of superstition he even had the whole deck changed. But his luck refused to part with him. He ordered champagne all round. They drank and dashed their glasses at the wall.

At a quarter to three the battle finally came to an end. The players rose to their feet.

Környey cried out:

'The benediction of St John!'

They filled their glasses with whatever remained – wine, schnapps, champagne. Ákos was busy cramming his winnings into his trouser pockets, jacket pockets, upper and lower waistcoat pockets, when he suddenly felt a stubbly chin on his cheek and a mouth pressing his lips with a long, slobbering kiss.

'My dear, dear old fellow!'

It was Ladányi, Sárszeg's 1848 delegate, who was now sobbing on Ákos's chest.

Ákos embraced him.

'You're a grand old forty-eighter, Laci, I know.'

'So are you, my dear old man,' said Ladányi, 'a good old Hungarian.'

And they wept.

Ákos suddenly picked up the tumbler full of schnapps they had set before him and downed it in one. The alcohol warmed its way through his body and lifted him to his feet. There was an enormous knocking in his old brain and he felt such delight that he really wouldn't have minded in the least if there and then, in this moment of giddy ecstasy, when he felt his whole being, his whole life, was in his grasp, he were to fall down and die on the spot.

His face was pale. He was a touch cross-eyed.

Noticing this, Környey turned to him and inquired:

'What is it, my dear Ákos?'

Ákos made no reply.

The schnapps he had just poured into himself gave him tremendous strength. He knew that he must leave at once, or he was done for. When he got out into the street outside the clubhouse, he felt all the independence of his youth returning to him. He swung left into Széchenyi Street and slipped away among the shadows of the walls.

He could hear them calling after him:

'Ákos!'

Then again, peremptorily, entirely without affection:

'Ákos!'

With ceremonious reproachfulness, they demanded his immediate return. The Panthers roared into the night.

What he had done was no joking matter. To sneak away without farewell was no less serious a crime than deserting one's post, leaving the flag in the mud. It was an act of betrayal, of insubordination, which the Panthers could not in any circumstances forgive, not even in the name of friendship.

Ignoring their cries, Ákos lengthened his stride and hurried resolutely homewards.

Suddenly he heard an explosion behind him. First one, then two, then three. They were firing their revolvers.

Then came another three shots, this time in quicker succession.

Ákos did not take fright. He knew this too belonged to the fun and games of a Thursday night, and that, in high spirits, Környey would always fire his revolver into the air. On one occasion he had shot the ceiling and mirrors of the Széchenyi to pieces. Completely without malice. Out of sheer abandon.

The citizens of Sárszeg knew this too. Whenever they awoke to such commotion on a Thursday night, they'd calmly roll over on their sides and murmur in their sleep:

'The Panthers are at it again.'

The Panthers gave Ákos a few minutes to respond to their alarm signals. Then, grumbling and cursing, they split into two groups. The first climbed back knock-kneed into the Széchenyi, while the second scurried off to seek out old Aunt Panna, whose little inn stayed open until dawn, serving wines that were celebrated throughout the county.

Ákos finally managed to disappear beneath the dark arches of the Town Hall. From here the cries of the Panthers sounded distant and muted. Only the odd loiterer staggered by, heavy with drink. Everyone drank in Sárszeg.

An old peasant stood swaying on the edge of the pavement. He attempted a few feeble steps, then fell flat on his face like a soldier struck by a bullet from behind. Toppled by the power of alcohol. And there, spread out on the battlefield, he remained.

Ákos was still sober enough to know that he was drunk. He ambled on stiffly, without swaying.

A few gas lamps glowed weakly through the gloomy night. The dry heat had finally broken. A vaporous humidity covered everything, heralding the approaching rainstorm. Shadows flitted across Széchenyi Square in the eerie light which fanned out from the arc lamp of the Baross Café, lending an uncertain, fantastical aspect to the Sárszeg night. Above, the illuminated yellow clock of the Town Hall glowed like a ripe melon.

On the terrace of the Baross Café young people were still eating ice cream. Ákos made his way towards them. He suddenly stopped in his tracks.

There on the terrace, beside a lavender bush, he spotted a young man in a fashionable new panama hat and a white summer suit leaning over a glass. Géza Cifra, on finishing his evening shift, had dropped in to listen to the Gypsy band.

He looked drearier than ever. His cold had now broken out in full force. Not only his left nostril was blocked, but the right one too, for his nose was even more sensitive than a tree frog to changes in the weather, and at times like these he could hardly draw any air at all. He breathed noisily through his mouth. Before him stood a glass of raspberry cordial and a straw.

Ákos observed him for some time. The youth appeared perfectly happy, with a look of self-satisfaction spread across his face that seemed to suggest complete disdain for the world. To Ákos even the innocent raspberry cordial, which he began to suck up through his straw, seemed like a pool of venomously strong, red schnapps.

So his little lordship is having fun, Ákos grumbled to himself with inexpressible hatred. If only he could knock that foppish panama from his head, with its fancy, dangling ribbon.

He turned red with rage, tensing the muscles in his puny arms.

He drew closer. Yes, he had the strength to do it now, to floor the boy with a single blow, to trample him underfoot, to strike him wherever he could, to tear his hair, gouge out his eyes, to kill him, kill him.

But what should he kill him with? He had only his pocket knife. He could make a scene at the very least. He walked over to Géza Cifra's table.

Ákos planted himself before the youth provocatively and offered no greeting.

Géza Cifra greeted him.

He removed his panama hat and sprang to his feet.

Ákos did not move. Then he plunged both hands into his trouser pockets to avoid shaking hands, and stretched his fingers out against the cloth. After a while he nodded meaningfully, then once again, a still deeper, more pronounced nod of the head.

'Do take a seat.'

Ákos took one more step forward. They were now so close their faces almost touched. Géza Cifra, who never drank at all, could smell the pungent schnapps on Ákos's breath.

'I won't take anything,' said Ákos sardonically. 'And I don't want anything either. I just wanted to see you.' And he lunged his whole torso derisively towards the youth.

'I'm most honoured. But please sit down.'

'I won't sit down,' said Ákos stubbornly. 'You just

go on amusing yourself,' he added, meaning something altogether different. 'Good night.'

'Well, good night then . . .' Géza Cifra stammered,
relieved that the conversation had come to an end and
he no longer had to think of what to say and how to
get away. 'A very good night to you, and my kindest
regards to your dear wife, good night.'

Ákos turned away without so much as a tip of his
hat. But on the pavement he stalled again and took
one more long, hard look at Géza Cifra, nodding as
before. The young man felt this, but didn't understand
what it meant. No longer daring to look back, he
turned his head, picked up the copy of the newspaper
Agreement, which lay in a wicker frame on the chair
beside him, and buried his whole body inside it.

Beside the spire of St Stephen's, the moon appeared
between the clouds as suddenly as if someone had
pressed a secret button. Its strong but dejected light
fluttered across the sleeping town. Ákos made his way
towards Bólyai Street.

He walked in the moonlight, his tilted bowler casting a thick shadow over his forehead. The greenish
haze reminded him of his last visit to Budapest, when
the doctors had instructed him to give up alchohol
and cigars, life's last pleasures, and he, on such a night,
had ambled back to his hotel room. And now, at this
daybreak hour, he fancied that he finally saw himself
as he really was, both now and in times gone by. He
saw the old bones which had served him for fifty-nine
years, and God only knew for how much longer. He
looked thoroughly, mortally sad.

Everywhere dogs were barking. Behind every fence, shaken from sleep by the restless moonlight. A moonlight chorus of yapping animals, howling with primal rage, throwing their weight back on their crooked, narrow hind legs, blinking up at the moon with short-sighted eyes, squinting at that mottled, porous, golden cheese they had been longing, for millennia, to wolf down from the sky.

At the corner of Bólyai Street, Ákos again heard the strains of Gypsy music. He thought the band must be following him. But no, they were bowing and scraping some way on ahead, at the house where Olga Orosz lived.

The Gypsies were performing a dawn serenade, lifted to the tips of their toes by their zeal.

Beneath the window, in which a light had just come on, stood Dani Kárász, István Kárász's son. A tear rolled down his cheek, as one had rolled down his father's cheek some hours before.

They had just struck up Mimosa's song, in honour of the prima donna.

Ákos, as he turned into Petőfi Street, attempted to whistle the tune, but couldn't. Instead he hummed Wun-Hi's song, the jovial, oriental ditty that began:

'Chin, Chin Chinaman . . .'

X

---

*in which, after several years in the making, the great
day of reckoning finally arrives, and our heroes
receive from life the solace and just deserts that come
to each and every one of us*

A drunkard never walks where he can fly.

Only the sober believe that the inebriate stagger to and fro. In reality they float on invisible wings and arrive everywhere much earlier than expected.

That time passes in between is of no consequence. For them time does not exist, and those who trouble themselves with such trifles are entirely deceived.

Nor shall the inebriate come to any harm, for the blessed Virgin carries them in her apron.

But opening the gate was another matter. Ákos spent ages fumbling with the key, turning it this way and that in the lock. But it still refused to budge. He wrestled still longer with the front door, before finally realising that it hadn't been locked at all.

He went inside, grumbling and cursing. Nothing in

his house was as it should be. Why, they could be robbed blind without even knowing, could lose everything they had.

Such disorder was, of course, exceptional.

What had happened was that, when the clock struck nine, his wife had started to worry. For as long as she could remember, her husband had always been home by this late hour. She went out into the street and squinted into the darkness to see if he was coming. On her way back inside she had forgotten to lock the door behind her.

Mrs Vajkay grew increasingly anxious. She couldn't imagine what might have happened.

She had been at home all day. After Ákos had gone to call in at the club for a quarter of an hour that afternoon, she had received two visitors. One was the washerwoman who had come to discuss the arrangements for washing day. The other was Biri Szilkuthy, Skylark's one and only close friend, a pretty young woman whose husband, a forester of sorts, had left her for a till girl at the Széchenyi Café. They were now suing for a divorce.

Biri Szilkuthy inquired after Skylark, with whom she had only recently grown friendly. The two of them would sit whispering for hours on the bench beneath the old horse chestnut tree.

Mother offered her a chocolate from the box Ákos had bought her at the theatre. They chatted and laughed, and by eight the box was empty.

When she had gone, the woman went into her daughter's room to do some sewing, spreading shirts and blouses over Skylark's unmade bed. She nervously popped a cube of sugar into her mouth, and sucked on it slowly. She looked at the pictures on the walls which she had seen so many times before. Dobozy and his betrothed, Batthyány, and the first Hungarian cabinet. Then she turned to the bronze-clasped photograph albums and leafed through three generations of Vajkays and Bozsós, ending with images of Skylark herself, at ten, at fourteen, with a doll, with a balloon, or sitting dreamily on a rock. But nothing could put her mind at rest.

She got up and went into the dining room, crossing the zigzag pattern of the machine-woven carpet, then hurried out into the hall and paced the full length of the coarse floor runner, which stretched all the way to the front door.

Here she was suddenly seized with fear. She flung open the doors of all the rooms, so that they all flowed into one. Then she switched on all the lights, even in the hall. A strong current of light flooded through the deserted house.

But in this light the silence seemed greater than ever. Nothing stirred. She waited to hear the rattle of a key in the lock. Silence. She listened for noises in the street. All was quiet. Only the creaking of floorboards as she paced to and fro. Then she stopped still.

She headed towards the bedroom. From the drawer of her husband's bedside table she took a key and hurried back through the gleaming house to the last room, the unused drawing room they kept for guests. It was there that the dusty, black piano stood. The old Bösendorfer had been a wedding present from her parents, a faithful piece of family furniture that had already served two generations, and had weathered many storms and charming soirees.

She sat down on the piano stool, rested her hands in her lap and meditated.

How long had it been since she last played? A long, long time. She had loved the piano once. She had even tried teaching Skylark, but, poor thing, she never got very far, simply didn't have the feel for it. When she was eighteen they had shut the lid, locking it with a little key to keep the room nice and tidy. And it had remained shut ever since. Even she had hardly touched it after that.

To while away the time she lifted the lid, which opened with a crack, and ran her stiff fingers down the keyboard. The keys were covered with a layer of cracked bone, not that much older than her own.

She knew only one tune by heart, a song from her girlhood, 'Upon the wavy Balaton . . .' And this she played now, somewhat feebly and desultorily, stopping every now and then. All the same it was soon over.

Then she sifted through the music books until she came across some Beethoven sonatas. She had a go at the first, whose daring, leaping shifts of tempo brought pangs of remembrance from the distant past. She had often played it in her twenties, on fine summer mornings. Now at first it didn't go too well. She put on her glasses to see the notes more clearly and repeated the piece until her fingers began to spin and

the steely, untuned piano resounded in melodic melancholy. She made a proper practice session of it, a veritable campaign. Over and over again, getting better
and better each time. On her face, which she held up
close to the music between two brightly burning
lamps, beamed an expression of strenuous concentration and wonder.

It must have been about three o'clock when she
finally felt exhausted. Without shutting the piano or
tidying away the music, she went straight to the bedroom. She didn't even put out the lights. Deciding to
wait no longer for her husband, she got into bed.

She had just pulled the quilt up over her shoulders
when she heard Gypsy music in the street nearby, followed by the barking of dogs. Soon she was sure she
could hear the clatter of the gate, a sound she had
already imagined so many times that evening. This
time, however, she was not deceived. She sat up in the
electric lamplight.

Ákos came into the bedroom.

'Father,' she said quizzically, in a voice that mixed
astonishment with reproach.

Her husband stood in the middle of the room. He
didn't even remove his hat, which sat crooked and
impertinent on his head. He no longer wore his
glasses. He had lost them somewhere along the way.

'What is it?' his wife asked faintly.

Ákos said nothing. He glared at the woman, the
smelly stump of a cigar still smouldering between his
teeth. No matter how he chewed at it, he couldn't
draw any smoke. He wore a surly scowl.

He's drunk, thought the woman suddenly. She was no less horrified by the thought, and by the apparition of the rigid, mysterious figure who stood before her, than if a complete stranger had broken into her bed-room in the dead of night.

She leaped out of bed. Without even reaching for her slippers, she ran over to prop her husband up.

'Sit down.'

'I'm not sitting down.'

'Then lie down.'

'I'm not lying down either.'

'What then?'

'I'm staying where I am,' Ákos stammered, leaning against the doorpost.

But then he did move.

He went as far as the table and slammed it hard with his palms.

'I'm staying where I am,' he growled menacingly. 'Just for that,' he repeated, 'I'm staying where I am.'

He was stubborn, like a child. His wife let him be.

'Fine, you stay where you are.'

'Matches!' he commanded.

The woman fetched the matches from the bedside table. Ákos lit up, sucking the flame into his crumbling cigar, which suddenly caught fire and singed his moustache. He spat left and right, ejecting the cigar from his mouth with his tongue and spitting once more after it on the floor.

Flecks of spittle sparkled white on the polished wooden floor.

'Cigar!' commanded Father.

His wife rummaged for his wallet in the breast pocket of his mouse-grey jacket and took out a cigar. Ákos bit off the end and lit up again.

Only now did she manage to coax the hat from his head and the cane from his hand. But still the man didn't move.

'You've had too much to drink,' said his wife with a conciliatory smile, as she tried to bring him to his senses. When she noticed that her husband had taken offence, she added softly, 'You've had a bit of a tipple, haven't you?' and she gazed at the man who stood before her, dead drunk.

The old man plunged his hands into his trouser pockets and rummaged. Suddenly he turned out both pockets.

Gold, silver and copper coins tumbled out, clattering and jangling across the floor, hiding themselves away under the furniture.

'Here you are,' Ákos shouted. 'Money!' He dug out another handful of coins. 'For the two of you,' and he dashed the money to the floor.

The coins screeched as they hit the ground.

Mrs Vajkay almost shrieked herself.

There was something deeply sinister about this confusion in her own orderly home, although she could not say why. They both detested gambling and had nothing but contempt for 'serious' card games.

The woman searched for the fallen coins which had rolled into dark corners and come to rest. All she asked was:

'Have you been playing cards?'

Ákos stared at her, then took a few deliberate and defiant steps forward to demonstrate how far he was from being drunk. He staggered all the way over to the bedside table. Here, however, he could keep his balance no longer and came to a complete standstill. With the cigar still burning in his mouth, he keeled over like a tree, landing face down on the bed.

'You'll burn the bedclothes,' Mother wailed. 'You'll set the whole house on fire.'

'What if I do?' Ákos growled. 'At least it would burn down. And we'd be rid of that too. Who cares?' he said sadly. 'Who cares?'

'Really, Ákos,' his wife interrupted, brushing the glowing ash from the quilt and pillows.

Somehow she managed to lift her husband to his feet. Again he had the cigar in his mouth and puffed vigorously as she hauled him over to the table. She slipped a chair beneath him and he sank into it.

'Honestly,' said the woman as she sat him down. 'What on earth's the matter?'

'With me?' asked Ákos with a shrug. 'What's the matter with me?'

'Yes, with you.'

'The matter with me,' he began, wiping away the ash that had fallen into his moustache, 'the matter with me,' he repeated in a deep and resolute voice, 'is that I'm a swine.'

'You?'

'Yes, me.' He nodded.

'What *are* you talking about?' the woman whined. 'You of all people, the sweetest – '

'Shut up!' the old man shouted. 'Hold your tongue. I'm a swine. A useless, miserable swine. That's what I am.'

The woman took pity on her husband and went over to embrace him. Ákos pushed her away.

'Leave me alone.'

'Nonsense,' said the woman, deep in thought. 'You a swine? Why on earth should you be a swine?'

'Because,' said Ákos, spitting out his second cigar, which had pinched his tongue with its caustic poison, 'because I am,' he repeated wearily.

Only now did his head really begin to spin. In this closed room, where yesterday's stagnant heat stood trapped, his drunkenness hit him with full force. His head fell to one side and he seemed to be nodding off. But his face grew increasingly pale. It made a picture of such frailty that his wife asked uneasily:

'Shall I make some tea?'

Ákos nodded.

The woman snatched up her crocheted shawl and ran as she was, barefoot, in her nightdress, into the kitchen, where, after clattering with pots and pans, she lit the stove. She boiled the kettle for tea.

Ákos sat in the armchair, almost motionless. He clasped the velvet armrests with both hands, for he felt the chair was rising slightly into the air. Only a couple of inches at first, but then higher, floating, foot by foot, all the way up to the ceiling and back, gaining speed as it went. Then it began to spin. It wasn't actually unpleasant, this spinning. Ákos found it quite amusing. He stared at the objects that hurtled past, the dancing mirror, the bow-legged doors, reeling all together in a tipsy waltz. He continually lost and regained consciousness.

In one such moment he managed to pull himself together. He stood up to get undressed. He pulled off his jacket and trousers, and tore off his necktie, whose clasp got caught on a button of his shirt. Drunk as he was, he still folded his clothes together neatly, with all the fussiness of old age, when the mind is increasingly preoccupied by ever more trivial details. He placed his watch, signet ring and keys in his wallet so that he'd be able to find them again in the morning and slip them back into his pockets, as he had done throughout the thirty-six years of his marriage.

His wife came in with the teapot, a mug and some rum.

'Drink this,' she said to her husband, who was already sitting on the bed undressed. 'You'll feel better in no time.'

Ákos filled the mug with rum, then splashed a drop of tea on top and stirred it in. The woman climbed into bed, shivering with cold from the kitchen.

The old man could only manage a few sips.

'Now come to bed,' said the woman.

And he would have done so, too, had he not been struck by the thought that always occurred to him before going to bed: that he should search the whole house for the hidden burglar he never found. In his shirt and underpants he tottered about in the dining room.

The chandeliers still burned. For a moment he didn't

know where he was. It was so light everywhere, out in the hall and in his daughter's bedroom too. He stubbornly staggered on to the drawing room.

Here he was greeted by still brighter light. At either end of the piano the two lamps, which mother had left on, still glowed, illuminating the keyboard, the open lid and the open scores strewn over the music rest.

Ákos burst out laughing, so heartily that his laughter echoed through the hollow house and all the way to the bedroom, where his wife, with knitted brows, tried to follow what was going on. Her husband soon returned.

'What happened here, then?' he asked in the same coarse tone he had used when he first came home. Once again he stood in the middle of the bedroom. 'What kind of nonsense have you been up to? Been having a ball, have we?' and he laughed so loud that he coughed, choking on his words.

'What are you laughing at?'

'You've been having a ball, haven't you?' Ákos repeated. 'A ball in this house? Have you been raising the roof, Mother?'

'I was waiting for you,' said the woman plainly. 'And I played the piano.'

'I bet you did,' said Ákos accusingly. 'You've been having a ball.' Then, accusingly, 'A ball.'

But he had hardly finished uttering these words when a sudden spasm seized his throat and he collapsed into the armchair, sobbing.

His dry sobs shook his whole body as he howled, without tears. He slumped forward across the table.

'Poor thing,' he moaned, 'poor thing. It's her I pity.'

He could see Skylark standing before him, just as in his dream. From behind a fence she stared at him like one possessed, begging him to help her. She was almost braying with grief.

'God, how I pity her, oh, God!'

'Why do you pity her?' asked the woman.

His wife wanted no part in this performance, even though she had the easier role to play. Though dazed by the unaccustomed lateness of the hour, she still had all her wits about her. She had neither witnessed her husband's dream nor read her daughter's letter, which had left such a deep impression on Ákos.

'You must never pity her,' said the woman, trying to placate her husband with cool, calm words. 'You've no reason to. She's been away. And she'll come back. She has to enjoy herself too, you know. Don't be so selfish.'

'How lonely she is,' Ákos whispered, gazing into space. 'How absolutely alone!'

'She'll be home tomorrow,' said Mother, affecting indifference. 'She'll be here tomorrow evening. And then she won't be alone, will she? Now come to bed.'

'Don't you understand?' the old man retorted heatedly. 'That's not what I'm talking about.'

'Then what are you talking about?'

'About what hurts right here,' and he beat his fist against his heart. 'About what's in here. Inside. About everything.'

'Come and get some sleep.'

'No,' Ákos replied bullishly, 'I refuse to sleep. I want to talk at last.'

'Then talk.'

'We don't love her.'

'Who doesn't?'

'We don't.'

'How can you say such a thing?'

'It's true,' Ákos cried, striking the table with his palms as before. 'We hate her. We detest her.'

'Have you gone mad?' the woman shouted, still lying in bed.

As if to provoke his wife still further, Ákos raised his voice, which already rasped and faltered.

'We'd much rather she wasn't here. Like now. And right now we wouldn't even mind if she, poor thing, were . . .'

He could not pronounce the terrible word. But this way it was yet more terrible than if he had.

The woman sprang out of bed and stood before him to put a stop to this enormity. She turned a deathly white. She wanted to make some reply, but the words stuck in her throat. For in spite of her frenzied indignation, she couldn't help wondering if her husband's outrageous suggestion might be true. She gaped at him, utterly astounded.

Ákos did not speak.

By now his wife was waiting to hear more. She almost longed for him to speak, to come out with everything at last. She sensed that the hour of reckoning had finally arrived. It was something she had often imagined, but never believed would really happen, least of all to her and at a time like this. She sat down in the armchair opposite, every part of her trembling. Yet she was still resolute, even a little curious. She did not interrupt when her husband began to speak again.

Ákos took up where he had left off.

'And wouldn't it be better? For her too, poor thing. And for us. Do you know how much she's suffered? Only I know that, with this father's heart of mine. What with one thing and another. The continual whispering behind her back, the laughter, the scorn, the humiliation. And we too, Mother, how much have we suffered? We waited one year, two years, hoping, as time passed by. We believed it was all a matter of chance. We told ourselves things would get better. But they only got worse. Always worse and worse.'

'Why?'

'Why?' echoed Ákos. Then, in the quietest of voices, he replied, 'Because she's ugly.'

The word had been uttered. Spoken for the first time. Then silence. A hollow silence resounded between them.

The woman leaped to her feet. No, this was not what she had imagined after all. Whenever they talked about her daughter, carefully avoiding this one issue, she always thought that one day they'd nevertheless return to it, to discuss it in greater detail, point by point, over several days perhaps, she and her husband, and maybe the odd relative. Béla, Etelka, a kind of committee almost, but not like this, not so openly, with such vulgar, prosaic simplicity. Her husband's words had put a sudden end to the possibility of any further argument or discussion. It hurt her, disgusted her, this merciless sincerity. Her husband had insulted a woman, had insulted her own flesh and blood. And, as if confronted by nothing more or less than this one insult, she cried out angrily, resentfully:

'No. No!'

'But yes. Yes! She's ugly. Frightfully ugly,' Ákos shouted, revelling in every word. 'Ugly and old, poor creature. Like this,' and he pulled the most hideous of faces. 'As ugly as I am.'

He struggled out of the armchair to reveal himself in his true light, and stood beside his wife.

Thus Skylark's aging parents stood face to face, barefoot, almost naked, with no more than a shirt between them. Two shrivelled bodies from whose embrace a daughter had once been born. They both trembled with emotion.

'You're drunk,' said the woman contemptuously.

'I'm not drunk.'

'It's blasphemy.'

'Even if she were lame,' Ákos roared, 'or a hunchback, or blind, she couldn't be uglier,' and now he was really crying; thick, hot tears washed his ash-smudged face, his tormented soul.

The woman, however, drew herself up to her full height.

'Enough,' she said suddenly, with an entirely unfamiliar severity of tone, and with such purpose in her eyes that she seemed a complete stranger. 'Enough!' and here she raised her voice. 'I absolutely forbid you to say such things about my daughter. She

is my daughter. Our daughter, and I have to defend
her against you. Shame on you!'

'What?' Ákos stammered, recoiling.

'I won't have it,' said the woman, beating her fist on
the table. 'I simply won't stand for it. You spoke of
nonsense earlier on. Well, here's your nonsense.'

Ákos awoke from his drunken stupor, as if the day
were beginning to dawn within him.

'All right then,' he conceded, 'let's be reasonable.
I'm a reasonable man, after all.'

'Well, you're not a bit reasonable right now. You
come home at all hours, turn the place upside down,
throw money all over the floor, try to set my house on
fire and then talk all kinds of nonsense. What you need
is a good night's sleep.' With that she made straight for
the bed.

'Mother,' said Ákos, calling her back. 'Stay a while
longer,' he begged.

The woman stopped still.

'What do you want?' she demanded. 'With all this
crying, all this shouting? I really can't understand you.'

Her voice was cold and stern.

She paused. Then, a little more gently:

'All right, so she won't marry. So what? Plenty of
girls remain single. She's thirty-five years old, someone may still come along. You never know. Just when
we least expect it. Do you want me to approach people
in the street? Or put an advertisement in the paper? For
a Vajkay girl? Come on, for heaven's sake.'

Mother stopped talking. Ákos waited for her to go

on. Her words did him good. The crueller the better. He wanted more, only harder, sharper.

After a while the woman continued:

'Or say she does get married. Just for the sake of argument. Suppose she does. To whoever proposes. Because there's always someone. Do you really think that marriage is such a heaven these days? Janke Hernád got married. Mrs Záhoczky told us all about it. How she came to the last Ladies' Society ball, her eyes red from weeping. Married some card-playing nobody who gambled the whole dowry away in half a year. And now where are they? Magda Proszner's husband beats her. Beats her, I tell you, and drinks. As for Biri Szilkuthy, you know her story. She was here today, pouring her heart out. Shame you didn't hear her. Is that what you want so badly? No, let her stay here with us. She'll never be as happy anywhere else. If that's God's will. After all, she's so used to us now.'

Out in the street, directly beneath their window, drunkards were whooping and bawling. Perhaps a group of Panthers, making their way through the night. They waited for the commotion to die down.

Mrs Vajkay pondered, always returning to the same point of departure.

'Ridiculous, the things you said. Hasn't she got everything she could possibly desire? She has nine dresses, two of which I've just had made for her. And five pairs of shoes. When she asked for that lovely blue feather boa last autumn, I bought it for her at once, even though it was frightfully expensive, fourteen forints. We've always given her all we could, haven't we, according to our means. It's true we had to economise here and there, but life is hard. And everything I've ever brought into this house is hers, her dowry, no one else so much as lays a finger on it. I set aside my every penny, and go on working in my old age, depriving myself of all good things so that she should have all she desires, the very best in life. And we brought her up well, didn't we? She finished school, I taught her the piano. I know she didn't take it very far, but everyone can see that she's an educated child. And look at her needlework. Most parents would be only too proud. Look at all these lovely tablecloths and doilies. All her own work. It was sinful what you said. Sinful and stupid.'

Now she seemed to rummage for something in her memory. There was a long pause before she continued:

'When she was five she fell down the attic steps and bumped her head. They thought she had concussion and a fractured skull. Remember, we even called the specialist from Pest. For two whole months I pressed that ice-cold chamois to her poor little head. I was utterly exhausted, nearly fell to pieces. And you accuse me? Even now I take her everywhere. She's my only friend. What would my life be like without her? All I know is that I love her, and couldn't love anyone more.'

Then she launched a new assault, turning to face her husband.

'And you love her too, Father. You love her very much. You can say what you like, you silly old thing.

When she fell that time, you yourself telegraphed for the doctor, running off at midnight like a madman. And you jumped for joy when the doctor said he'd no longer be needed. And think of all you did last year when she had that upset stomach. It was always you who took her to school, even when she was a big girl. And if she wasn't back by exactly half past twelve you were always scared she'd been run over. You bought her all those thick, warm clothes, so she shouldn't catch cold, and it was you who made her wear those awful thick stockings, poor thing. You were frightfully funny, you know. Your daughter and I had a right old laugh at you. Ah, the giggles we had together. Isn't that so?'

Ákos smiled wearily.

'But that's not the problem,' the woman continued. 'The real problem is that you avoid people. Recently you've grown quite unsociable, a proper little hermit. But one can't just shut oneself away like we do. She'd like to go out more, too, only she never says so. It's because of you that she hides at home. She always thinks you'd be annoyed, that's why she doesn't suggest going anywhere. And she wouldn't want to go without you. But you can see how people like her and respect her – Környey, Priboczay, Feri Füzes and even . . .' Here she paused for thought. 'Well, everyone. Let's make up our minds to go out at least once a week. And to take her with us. If you never show yourself, they just forget you. All we need is a bit of variety. Then everything will be different. All right?'

Ákos was glad to be overpowered by the force of

argument. And now that his wife had plunged to the very depths of cheerful absurdity, he threw his hand in and happily surrendered.

'Why don't you say anything?' urged his wife.

The old man was no longer in need of consolation. He had finally sobered up. He felt sleepy, and the soles of his feet were freezing on the cold floor.

At last emerging from the storm which had whipped up his blood, he slowly made his way to the bed and lay down, thoroughly exhausted.

It was good to lie down, if only because he no longer had to face his wife. He was ashamed of his earlier outburst, his sentimental, pusillanimous verbosity, which would make any man in his right mind blush. With the quilt pulled high over his chin, he really seemed to be hiding in bed. He waited to see what would happen next.

His wife, however, had run out of things to say. She just sat there, motionless, in her armchair.

Now she would have liked her husband to speak, to confirm or deny what she had said. She waited for fresh words, new points of view, which would either support her own or refute them for good. For however forcibly she had spoken, inside she wasn't at all convinced of what she had said. In the structure, the architecture, of her agile speech for the defence, with all its cunningly contrived sighs, inflections and crescendos, she nevertheless felt she had left a gap somewhere, a crack that still needed filling. But Ákos did not echo the well-meaning torrent of words to which he had yielded.

Thus the woman remained alone, tormented by still more painful thoughts than the man she had consoled. She stood up, as if somehow looking for help, for herself, for him, for all of them. All kinds of things occurred to her, all kinds of people; even, for one short moment, Miklós Ijas, who had seemed so sympathetic the other day.

But she immediately swept the thought from her mind. He was no more than a boy, hardly twenty-four years old.

Ákos lay in silence.

It was left to the woman to speak again. As if she were talking to herself, summing up all that had gone before.

'We love her very much,' she insisted. 'Both of us. And even if we loved her a thousand times more, we still . . .'

'Still what?' Ákos prompted, lifting the quilt from his mouth in genuine curiosity. 'What could we still do?'

'We still – ' Mother sighed. 'Could we still do more?' she asked.

'That's just it,' replied Ákos dully, in a voice devoid of hope. 'What more could we do? Nothing. We've done all we can.'

All we can, the woman thought. Everything humanly possible. We've endured everything.

And she looked about her. But Ákos was silent again.

Now she could see that she stood alone – alone in the room, alone in the world, alone with her pain. And her heart was wrung with such despair that she almost collapsed.

But then her gaze involuntarily wandered towards the ebony crucifix that hung on the wall above their conjugal bed.

From the black wooden base hung the dear, tortured body, modelled from cheap plaster. The bony ribcage, the chest which tumbled forward ravaged with pain, and the hair, thickly matted with deathly perspiration, all glittered in their coating of thin gold leaf.

On the boundary between life and death, this swooning Son of God had watched over them for decades. He, who heard their every word and observed their every gesture, who saw into the darkest corners of their hearts, must have surely seen that they weren't lying now.

He flung open His arms upon the cross, exalting human suffering in a single, heroic gesture that belonged to Him alone since the beginning of time. But His head dropped, anticipating the numb indifference into which it was about to fall, His face already petrified with pain. Even He could not extend the woman a helping hand.

But His presence was powerful all the same. Something real, something immense, in this provincial room, where everything was so tiny. He, who had come into the world to help the wretched, had died for those who suffer, radiated the glorious light of global historical tragedy, the brilliant, burning light of eternal love.

The woman took one step towards the crucifix. And

now, for the first time, the tiniest of teardrops glistened in her eyes.

Again it was she who spoke.

'We must pray, Father,' she said, mainly to herself. 'We must have faith in God, in Christ the Saviour. I pray all the time. Whenever I wake up in the night and can't get back to sleep, I always pray. And then my heart is unburdened and I can sleep again. We must pray, Father, pray and have faith. God will help her. And He'll help us too.'

To this Ákos said nothing. Not that he disagreed with his wife. He was a deeply religious man, especially since he had turned forty, a devout Catholic who went to confession every Easter and took the holy sacrament. But the men of Sárszeg hid their religious faith, as they hid their tears, behind a veil of pious modesty. Only the women displayed their piety, and were fully expected to do so.

Mother put out the light and got into bed. She too pulled the quilt up over her chin.

Nothing had been settled or resolved. But at least they had grown tired. And that was something.

For some minutes they were silent.

Then Ákos sat up in bed.

'You know what?' he said meaningfully. 'I saw him again.'

The woman knew at once whom he meant.

'Did you?'

'Sitting in the Baross Café. He said hello.'

'And you?'

'Me too. So he wouldn't think anything. He'd been drinking.'

'So he drinks now, does he?' She pursed her lips.

'I always told you,' said Ákos, 'that he'd end up rotten. He was in a bad way. He hasn't long to live.'

They'd been discussing Géza Cifra's lack of colour, haggardness and secret illnesses for years, always setting new dates for his imminent demise: come March, come October. But the little railway official still went on living, with his boorish friends, his eternal colds and incurable complaints. Ákos brooded.

'Though the mills of God grind slowly . . .' he added, and lay back down in bed.

Then he sat up again.

'There's a fire down below,' he said jovially.

His stomach burned, mercilessly, all the way up to his throat. He swallowed a spoonful of bicarbonate of soda, but so clumsily that it sprinkled over his nightshirt and dusted his chin. He chewed the white powder with his discoloured teeth.

They didn't light the nightlight. But even without it the room wasn't dark. Light filtered in through the chinks in the lowered shutters, casting bright, shimmering wavelets on the walls. From the street the rattle of peasant carts on their way to market could already be heard.

Dawn was breaking.

XI

_____

in which there is mention of getting up late, of rain,
and in which the Panthers reappear

Those rakish metropolitans, who live by night and sleep by day in carefree capitals, are used to waking in the dark and meeting once again the selfsame night from which they parted company the day before.

This is their black dawn. It doesn't frighten them or take them by surprise. They greet it with a stretch and a yawn, lighting the lamp with sleepy hands, hurrying into the bathroom to wash and shave, then dressing quickly in front of the wardrobe, before stepping out refreshed into the dimly lit street. The people who pass before them here are weary from their daily round. Many long hours are already behind them, endless discussions and disputes, a hastily snatched breakfast and a guzzled lunch. Now only dinner stands between them and their beds. They move more slowly, speak more softly, visibly disillusioned with the day now drawing to a close. A hackney carriage jolts past,

pulled by an exhausted horse, which had still been able
to gallop that morning. A baleful lethargy hovers in
the air. But this does not dishearten the new arrivals,
fresh from sleep. It makes them all the more conscious
of their own high spirits and hopes. They pass among
their fellow men with a spring in their step, leaving
them way behind in unfair competition. They laugh at
the electric light, remembering the bright sunshine on
which they had turned their backs, they swagger with
vitality, and effortlessly, blithely, almost maliciously
turn into the marble-laden foyer of some garishly lit
bar where, summoned either by passion or profession,
they take up where they left off the day before.

But for those who have never lived like this, and
have always risen early, somewhere in the country,
such late awakenings bring nothing but anxiety, sad-
ness and remorse.

As they look up at the still dark window, they think
it is not yet dawn and want to go on sleeping into this
second night, as if it were still the first.

Their bodies are not fully rested from their daytime
sleep. Then suddenly they remember everything. All
the extraordinary events of the night before: the spinning of cards, glasses, words, the new direction their
lives had suddenly seemed to be taking, before they
felt compelled to flee, without fully understanding
what had happened, driven by the spectre of time ill
spent and a sense of obligation to make amends for
their transgressions, to return to their duties and settle
back into the old routine. They rise giddily, unable
at first to recognise their rooms, their most intimate

possessions, the street in which they live. It is as if everything were coated with a thin layer of soot. They haven't seen the sun, which has, in the meantime, burned to a cinder. They haven't greeted the day, which, without their knowing, has completely blackened, leaving only the odd flying ashes and clinkers behind as a disquieting surprise. They don't know whether they are hungry or full, hot or cold. Thus they flounder until they find their proper place in space and time, and only then do they notice that their heads are spinning and sore.

The woman, who first opened her eyes late in the afternoon, towards five, was tortured by such feelings. She was the first to wake. Her husband went on sleeping.

She slipped carefully out of bed, put on her thick flannel dress and wrapped her head in a scarf. She got on with the cleaning like some elderly servant. Dustpan and brush in her hands, she shuffled from room to room.

The lamps still burned by the piano, having kept their vigil night and day. The woman reproached herself for the senseless waste of electricity.

She had much to do. During the week they had often moved the furniture from one room to another. Now she had to sort it all out again and put each piece back where it had stood for decades. She spent a long time searching for Skylark's needlework, the tablecloth under which she had left the pantry key. When it finally turned up she spread it over the marble plinth of the mirror and pressed it flat with the two bronze-clasped photograph albums. She looked around for any more incriminating evidence. Now she only had to tidy up the piano, clear away the music and lock the lid. She took the key into the bedroom and gave it to her husband, who had just woken up.

Here she went down on her knees and scrubbed the dirty, spittle-flecked parquet, sweeping away the cigar ash and gathering up the coins and banknotes which lay strewn all over the floor. She rattled and clattered as she cleaned. The noise drove Ákos out of bed. He dressed briskly. He spoke of indifferent matters.

'What time is it?'

'Half past six.'

Looking in the mirror he saw the traces of bicarbonate of soda still clinging to his chin. He looked away. This morning's scene struck him as childish and tasteless. He didn't mention it at all. Nor did his wife.

'Dark, isn't it?'

'Yes, it's already late. The train will soon be in.'

'It's cold.'

'Yes, it's raining outside.'

The woman opened the shutters and aired the room. A cold, unfriendly stream of air swept the stuffy room, fluttering the curtains.

It was raining.

They could hear the whistle of the wind and the creaking of signboards. The rain spluttered through the glass bulbs of the gas lamps. Damp, round umbrellas swelled. People squelched through puddles in mud-spattered trousers, grimacing as they locked their umbrellas in battle with the storm. The tin mouths of the drains spewed foamy water which gushed in streams into the overgrown ditches of Petőfi Street. A paraffin lamp already smouldered in Mihály Veres's dark, unhealthy workshop.

They both observed this scene for some moments.

'It's autumn,' said Ákos.

'Yes,' said the woman. 'It really is autumn.'

They shut the windows.

'You'll have to take your autumn coat,' she said then. 'Otherwise you'll catch your death. And an umbrella too.'

'Do hurry up,' Ákos urged.

'I am hurrying.'

It was no small task to make everything as it should be, the five rooms, the hall, after a week of disorder.

They stumbled to and fro and the harder they worked the longer it seemed to take them.

It was nearly half past seven. Ákos picked up the umbrella and opened it out in the room to make sure the framework hadn't rusted. He pulled on his old, nut-brown overcoat which dangled loosely front and back and made him look rather thin.

They were just about to leave when he suddenly crouched to the floor. By the back leg of the wardrobe he had caught sight of a gold coin. He picked it up and gave it to his wife.

'Put this away.'

Then, when they reached the street, it was the woman's turn to stop short.

'Wait,' she said. 'I'll take this back inside,' and she

pointed to her new crocodile handbag. 'I don't really want it now. Not with this.'

Ákos nodded.

The wind howled. It crashed into the old man, spun him round and tried to wrench the umbrella from his hand. It blew impertinently into his face and completely took his breath away. It lifted the woman too, as she came hurrying after her husband. They climbed into a carriage.

The station stood deserted. There was not a soul in sight.

The rain quickened, streaming down the sides of the dirty carriages which were thick with summer dust. In the distance a few green flames flickered above the empty track. Coal smoke drifted everywhere and the satanic smell of sulphur filled the air.

It was after half past eight, but not a single handbell had sounded. Darkness descended over the warehouses.

Only from the window of the telegraph office came the glow of lamplight. Here in happy seclusion, protected from the droning wind and rain, sat the telegraphists in idyllic calm, bent over their desks like fantastic silkworm breeders, winding into spools the long, white threads that bound the whole world tightly into one. In the freight sheds porters leaned back on rough, wooden boxes daubed with all kinds of figures and letters scribbled gloomily in tar.

The Vajkays sat down at a neatly laid table in the glass-roofed station portico.

After nine, Géza Cifra came in from the station

manager's office, whose door creaked noisily on rusty hinges as he entered. He must have been standing in for someone as he was doing the evening shift again.

He wore a heavy autumn coat and hurriedly rolled the red armband with the winged wheel insignia over his sleeve. He held a handkerchief to his mouth, so as not to inhale the musty air, and wiped his nose.

He was very pale. No doubt he too had gone to bed at dawn.

In the steamy air his profile seemed almost demonic. Mrs Vajkay felt he'd be capable of anything: deception, corruption, maybe even murder. And he looked so ill. She could hardly recognise him at all. The old couple exchanged glances, diagnosed the worst and, with a silent nod, buried the boy once more. By March, at the latest, it would all be over.

He hurried over to them, if only to clear the air after yesterday's misunderstanding, or simply to know its cause and see how the land now lay. With a croupy voice he inquired:

'Is she coming today?'

'Yes.'

'Then there's plenty of time,' and he took out his pocket watch as was his wont. 'The Tarkő train is two and a half hours late.'

He offered this information quite indifferently and then withdrew. For the Vajkays, however, the news was anything but indifferent.

'I hope nothing's wrong,' said Ákos, almost inaudibly.

'I shouldn't think so,' his wife replied in the same whisper.

'Then why's it so late?'

'You heard him. He didn't say.'

'You should have asked him.'

'Yes.'

'Perhaps I should send a wire.'

'Where to?'

'That's true. The train's already on its way.'

But Ákos rose to his feet all the same. Leaving his umbrella behind, he staggered out among the tracks, tottering over the wet gravel to find someone who could provide a reassuring answer to his questions. He splashed about in the pouring rain. But the porters were already snoring on their wooden benches, fast asleep. Beside the engine room he came across a grumpy, dirty workman carrying an iron bar and pincers. Ákos asked him why the train was delayed.

'It'll turn up,' the workman replied. 'Give it time.'

'There hasn't been an accident, has there?'

'That I can't say.'

Ákos stared at the decrepit workman, thinking of the heartless agitators he had read about in the paper.

'Go down to the end and turn right,' the man suggested.

Ákos went down to the end and turned right. Then he turned left. Then right again. But still he found no one. Even Géza Cifra had disappeared somewhere inside.

It was the first day of autumn. Everyone had stayed at home.

Only Mrs Vajkay waited on the platform.

Ákos returned to her, soaked to the skin.

'Did you find out anything?'

'Nothing.'

He sat back down at the table. Nausea climbed his throat, all the way up to his mouth. He swallowed repeatedly, his head thumping. He thought he was going to faint, fall reeling from his seat and die, then and there, on the spot. He was overcome by a hideous sense of disgust. He felt like collapsing against the iron pillars which supported the portico, then throwing himself to the ground. But he held back. He had to wait until she arrived.

'Are you unwell?'

'A little.'

'Perhaps you should order something.'

They rang for the waiter.

The waiter replied effusively to their questions, entertaining them with a most detailed account of a railway accident that had occurred some years before. He prattled on relentlessly like the rain.

They ordered cold milk.

Ákos removed his hat to clear his head in the cool air. The tight leather gusset had left a narrow streak of violet on his forehead. Only now could one see what had become of him. His skin had crumpled like paper, and his face was as white as chalk. The extra weight he had put on at the King of Hungary over the last few days had vanished, together with the genial, ruddy glow on his face. Once again he was gaunt, sickly and pale, just as he had been when his daughter had departed.

'Take a sip. It's nice and cool.'

As Ákos drank he thought:

'Railway accident.'

The woman, for her part, thought:

'The train isn't late. Something else has happened.'

The old man imagined – and a number of suspicious signs confirmed his presentiment – that the train had crashed somewhere, only they didn't dare say so and were keeping it quiet. He could see the heap of carriages before him, and the bleeding, choking bodies beneath the ruins. Later he became more inclined to believe that the train had merely been derailed and stood stranded in some open field, where, in the dark and rainy night, it was raided by all kinds of wicked highwaymen. He vacillated between these speculations, giving credence first to one, then to the other. His wife, on the other hand, stuck to her initial conviction: the train had already arrived, hours ago, perhaps before they had reached the station, or later, and they simply hadn't noticed it. Their daughter had looked for them and then gone on without them. Perhaps she had gone straight home, or perhaps she had travelled on somewhere, to some entirely unknown place where they'd never find her again.

She could not explain these thoughts, nor understand how she could possibly have missed her daughter. But her doubts, though less horrific than her husband's, tormented her all the more, precisely because they were so mysterious and obscure.

In the meantime, however, they went on talking.

'Feeling better?'

'A little.'

'What's the time?'

'Past ten.'

By now the station had at last begun to come to life. The rain subsided, and by a quarter past ten quite a crowd had gathered to meet the Budapest express.

Meeting this train was a favourite pastime of the Sárszeg intelligentsia, whether they were expecting anyone or not. They simply came to observe the passengers and, for a few short moments, to immerse themselves in the alluring glamour of metropolitan life.

The Budapest express rolled in on time, and, to the delight of its devoted Sárszeg audience, the enormous engine let out a shriek and a whistle, accompanied by a fountain of sparks, as if extemporising a festive firework display.

This was of no interest to Ákcs and his wife.

They scrutinised the alighting passengers, as if the one they sought could possibly be among them.

Haughty Budapesters arrived wrapped in splendid shawls and carrying pigskin suitcases. A porter from the King of Hungary relieved them of their luggage with a bow, before escorting them to the restaurant's own bright, glass-encased berlin, in which they were transported to where a hot meal and a clean room awaited them.

Those who were continuing their journeys did not look out upon the insignificant station for long. At most they opened a tiny gap in the curtains, which they immediately shut again with a sneer. By one window a foreign-looking lady stood in the electric light, furnished with every imaginable European comfort and a scarf around her neck, gazing at the rusty pump well and the geraniums in the station manager's window. What a godforsaken hole, her expression seemed to suggest. In the kitchen of the dining car the red-faced chef briefly appeared before the window in a white cap, laughing heartily at some joke.

Now the Vajkays' panic reached fever pitch.

In a state of excitement, things that normally pass unnoticed can seem pregnant with significance. At such times even inanimate objects – a lamppost, a gravel path, a bush – can take on a life of their own, primordial, reticent and hostile, stinging our hearts with their indifference and making us recoil with a start. And the very sight of people at such times, blindly pursuing their lonely, selfish ends, can suddenly remind us of our own irrevocable solitude, a single word or gesture petrifying in our souls into an eternal symbol of the utter arbitrariness of life.

Such was the effect of the laughing chef on the elderly couple.

As soon as they saw him, they not only suspected, but knew for certain that they were waiting in vain and that the night would pass without their ever seeing their daughter. They were now convinced she would never arrive.

And it wasn't only they who were waiting now.

Everyone and everything around them became a personification of waiting itself.

Objects stood still. People came and went.

Towards the west, billowing, ink-black clouds engulfed the sky.

Among those who admired, from beginning to end, the arrival and departure of the Budapest express was Bálint Környey. He greeted Ákos with a roar of laughter.

'You gave us the slip,' he said reproachfully. 'You wily old Panther, you left us in the lurch. What time did you get home?'

'Around three.'

'So you got a good night's sleep,' said Környey, yawning into his gloved hand. 'We upped sticks about nine in the morning.'

He pointed at the milk.

'I see you've fallen back into depravity.'

'I have a headache,' said Ákos.

'Take my advice,' said the old sinner with a wink. 'Waiter, a tankard of beer. Well, old boy, what do you say?'

'No, I daren't. Not a drop. Never again.'

No sooner had the tankard arrived than Környey gulped down the sparkling, cool beer into the bottomless pit of his stomach.

Naturally the Panthers followed on behind him, some ten of them who had come straight from the club, where, at six that afternoon, they'd had pork marrow and pickled cucumbers with a bottle or two of red wine. They joined Környey at the Vajkays' table to drink beer. Priboczay and good old Máté Gaszner, Imre Zányi in his top hat and Szolyvay, who wore an old-fashioned cape against the cold. Feri Füzes was there too, with his sickly smile, along with Judge Doba, who sat smoking a Virginia and didn't say a word.

The most valiant among them was Szunyogh, who hadn't even been to bed at all. He had passed out for a couple of minutes at dawn, but, in accordance with ancient custom, they had stretched him out on the table with two candles at his head and sung the '*Circumdederunt*'. At this he had come to his senses. Since then he had marched from one inn to the next drinking nothing but schnapps.

Now, too, he dismissively pushed aside the tankard of beer that stood before him.

'*Etiam si omnes, ego non.*'

And he ordered schnapps instead.

'*Aquam vitae, aquam vitae.*'

By now he could speak only Latin, above all through quotations from the classics. At times like these he'd rattle off whole pages of Virgil and Horace. The alcohol set his sharp wits alight and he didn't appear drunk in the least. He sat erect, his blue eyes sparkling brightly, and seemed the most sober of them all. His thick, red nose, which had bled that afternoon, was stuffed with yellow cotton wool he had been given for this purpose by the chemist.

After the third glass of schnapps, Priboczay could not resist performing his ancient party trick. He lit a match and carefully held it in front of Szunyogh's lips.

'Look out,' said several of the Panthers at once. 'He'll explode. He'll go up in flames.'

Completely unruffled, Szunyogh stared calmly into space.

'*Castigat ridendo mores,*' he muttered.

Those versed in Latin shouted back at him:

'*Vino veritas*, old boy, *vino veritas.*'

The prank delighted Feri Füzes in particular.

He was Szunyogh's former pupil and had often come a cropper with his appalling Latin. He always leaped at any opportunity to pique the old man, as if in repayment of a long-standing debt. For want of a better idea of his own – Feri Füzes could never count to two in his ideas, and the one idea he could count to was usually someone else's – he too lit a match and, in the hope that what had worked once would work twice, lifted it to Szunyogh's mouth.

Szunyogh, however, blew out the match with a single breath and knocked it from his hand.

Everyone applauded. Everyone except Feri Füzes.

'Excuse me,' he said sharply.

'*Si tacuisses, philosophus mansisses.*'

'I beg your pardon?' asked Feri Füzes attempting to affect a certain gentlemanly sang-froid, but unable to disguise the embarrassment of a poor pupil.

He looked his former teacher contemptuously up and down, then drew closer towards him.

'*Silentium,*' Szunyogh cried, raising a trembling finger and staring straight through this small-time cavalier with unspeakable contempt. '*Silentium,*' he repeated, now only to himself as he sank enraptured into that deep and peaceful stillness which he would soon inhabit for good. '*Silentium.*'

Feri Füzes sat back down and debated whether or not to send his seconds to the old drunkard the following day.

The day had passed, for the Panthers, much like any other Friday. Most of the day they spent lying stretched out on their couches, fully clothed, recovering from the night before. The wives sat at home, nursing their patients. For lunch they prepared cabbage broth and caviar puree with lemon and onion. They opened bottle after bottle of mineral water and beer, the latter, as is well known, being the perfect antidote to alcohol poisoning.

Only at around eleven in the morning would the men pay a brief call on Priboczay, who, as a fellow reveller and time-honoured Panther, prepared expert cures for their various complaints in the St Mary Pharmacy. According to the individual taste and ailment of each patient, he mixed medicines from a whole range of ingredients. He took down the *Tinctura China, Tinctura Amara* and *Tinctura Gentiana*, and poured them into handsome cut-glass beakers, stirring in the odd drop of *Spiritus Mentha* and more volatile oils from smaller vials, before baptising the whole concoction with a final dash of ether. This final touch was never to be skimped.

Szunyogh received an extra dose of unadulterated ether, and much good it did him.

The others stood in a circle, chinked their glasses and knocked back the bitter potions. Screwing up their mouths and wrinkling their noses, they all emitted a single, simultaneous Brr. In an instant they were as right as rain.

Now Környey sonorously requested leave to speak.

He had much to report: who had collapsed and when; who had arrived home at what hour and in what manner – on foot, in a carriage, alone or aided by the Samaritan committee whose charge it was to transport the more paralytic Panthers to their beds like corpses; then who had been drinking wine, champagne or schnapps, and how much of each had been consumed by whom; and finally who had been sick and how many times. For in Sárszeg this served as the surest measure of a good time. Those who were sick twice had had a better time than those who were sick only once. Yesterday some had even been sick three times. These had enjoyed an exceptionally good night.

Towards dawn, when they had all soaked up as much of Aunt Panna's wines as they could take, Környey suddenly raised the alarm and called out the fire brigade, who, at his command, hosed down the whole company. From there they thundered off on a fire engine to the last station of their revelry, the Turkish bath, sounding the siren as they went.

Werner was with them too, the tongue-tied Austrian lieutenant rifleman, who when the least bit tipsy couldn't even speak Moravian but was a charming fellow all the same. In the Turkish bath he flatly refused to get undressed, yet insisted on bathing nevertheless. In his yellow-buttoned military greatcoat and cap, his sword by his side and gold stars on his lapels, he waded into the steaming hot water. To the cheers of his admirers, who greeted him like a real hero, he ardently drew his sword, saluted, and with stiff, ceremonious parade steps marched out of the pool just as he had marched in, proceeding through the entrance hall and out into the street. The water streamed from his greatcoat and, as he receded through the early-morning air, he disappeared inside an enormous cloud of steam. The whole scene was so indescribably humorous and ingenious that it deserved to be commemorated in the Panthers' records, which were kept by Feri Füzes.

Környey spared no detail in his elaborate account of events, which he delivered with all the precision of a conscientious historian preserving crucial data for posterity. At times his audience roared and shook with laughter, but even this could not conceal their pallor.

Meanwhile others joined them too, complete strangers who made themselves quite at home at the table. A birdlike ham actor, no doubt some member of the chorus, who looked rather like a starling, extended his hand to Ákos.

'Hello, old chap.'

'Hello, old chap,' Ákos replied, shaking hands.

'Who was that?' his wife inquired.

'I don't know,' said Ákos.

There were plenty of such characters, with whom Ákos had been on first-name terms during the feverish festivities of the previous evening. Now, however, he had no idea of who they were.

The whole table seemed a haze before him. The

longer he observed the wilting heads and faded faces, above all those of Szunyogh and Doba, the more he felt he must be dreaming the whole thing, sitting among deathly shadows like a ghost.

It was Környey, who had already downed two tankards of beer, who kept the conversation going, throwing one cigarette end after the other on the stone floor, never running out of things to say. His voice sounded like a droning wasp in the Vajkays' ears. Neither the old man nor his wife could bear to listen.

Ákos repeatedly glanced at his pocket watch.

'Are you waiting for someone?' asked Környey suddenly.

'My daughter.'

'She's been away?'

'For a week now.'

'I had no idea. Where?'

'To Béla's, on the plain.'

'And she's back today?'

'Yes, today.'

The Panthers made ready to leave.

The woman explained to Feri Füzes:

'She went for a break, you see.'

'A change of air,' said Feri Füzes, the perfect conversationalist. 'And very healthy too.'

'But the train's so terribly late. My husband and I are frightfully worried. It was supposed to arrive at eight twenty-five, but there's still no sign of it.'

'Good Lord,' said Feri Füzes, 'it's already half past eleven.'

'I hope nothing's wrong,' Mrs Vajkay went on nervously.

'That I can't say, my dear lady,' replied Feri Füzes correctly, whom no circumstance could sway from uttering the truth, not even the pleas of a gentlewoman. 'I've really no idea.'

He wasn't even particularly interested. Having never concerned himself directly with the Vajkays' specific affairs of honour, there was really no further information he could supply. All he added was:

'We must hope for the best. I kiss your hand.'

With that, he took up his hat, withdrew with a sickly smile, and followed the other Panthers, who, with Környey at the fore, were already making their way out of the station. And now, after so many noble adventures and entertainments – or, as Szunyogh put it, *post tot discrimina rerum* – the Panthers finally headed home to bed.

XII

---

*in which the author describes the joys of arrival and
reunion*

Ákos was once again left alone with his wife.

His disquiet had reached the point where the
anxiety born of self-reproach subsides, and
speculation is replaced by a dumb stupor which can
only mumble broken, meaningless words. He no
longer thought of anything, no longer imagined what
had happened and what still might happen. He only
breathed the odd sigh to keep his fears alive.

'If only she were here!'

'She'll be here soon.'

'If only the Good Lord will help us one more time.'

'He will. He will.'

Mother, who was no less anxious, smiled reassur-
ingly at her husband and gave him a hand to squeeze.
Both their hands were ice cold. Everything seemed so
hopeless.

In an attempt to outwit their fears, they busied
themselves with trivial questions and disputes. Where

had they put the pantry key, had they locked the study door?

Then the signal bell rang.

They shuddered at the sound. They stood alone on the platform, for after the departure of the Panthers the station had completely cleared. The waiters had taken up the tablecloths.

Behind them, chugging along at a leisurely pace on the outer track, a long mixed freight and passenger train pulled in, with endless wagonloads of canvas-covered boxes, petrol drums and livestock. They heard a dull, repeated whistle in the darkness from where the passengers soon began to emerge from the third-class carriages; simple folk, peasants with bundles, market women with fruit baskets balanced on their heads, rummaging awkwardly in their bosoms for their tickets by the exit gate.

Géza Gifra informed the couple that this was still not the Tarkő train, which was, however, only one station down the line, and would be in any minute now.

He was right.

Just when they least expected it, the little coffee grinder appeared on the horizon, the same engine they had seen off one week before.

Like a pair of bloodshot eyes, its two red lamps strained at the track through the darkness. It approached with caution, feeling its way, so as not to step on anyone's feet. The engine grew larger by the minute. It had been washed a bright black by the rain, and kept coughing and sneezing as if it had caught cold. The brakes whined, the carriages moaned. It was hardly the most uplifting of sights.

Jolting over the points, it seemed to hobble along until suddenly, quite unexpectedly, it veered to the right and swung towards them on the inner track. It seemed unwilling to come to a halt and dragged its load towards the engine house until the very last carriage finally came to a standstill before their noses.

The Vajkays rushed towards the carriage.

Ákos couldn't see too clearly and automatically reached for his pocket, only to remember that his spectacles had gone missing the night before and he'd have to buy a new pair.

Only one arc lamp now burned above them, rendering the darkness still more uncertain.

In addition to this, there was an almighty din. The quarrelsome cries of passengers calling for porters became entangled with the twilight.

The eyes and ears of the elderly couple were equally confused. Unable to focus their flagging attention on the dizzying scene, they locked their gazes on to the one carriage that stood immediately before them. From this a horse dealer alighted, followed by a tall woman with her husband, whom they didn't recognise. After them came two elderly gentlemen and finally a young couple, carrying their little son together in their arms as he slept sweetly in a cheap, straw hat with green tassels. The carriage was now completely empty.

There was no longer any movement at the front end of the train either. Most of the passengers were already

handing their tickets to the inspector at the gate, who
kept repeating:

'Tickets, please. Tickets.'

Luggage was being wheeled away on trolleys.

'I can't see her,' said Ákos.

The woman made no reply.

If only to steady herself, she then said in an under-
tone:

'Perhaps she missed it and will come tomorrow.'

Had these doubts lasted a second longer, it would
have been the end of them both.

But far away in the darkness, with a wavering,
almost ducklike waddle, a woman was approaching.
She wore a black oilskin hat, not unlike a swimming
cap, and a long, almost ankle-length, transparent,
waterproof cape. In her hand she held a cage.

They stared at her blankly. Terrified of another disappointment, they didn't dare believe it was she. They
didn't recognise the oilskin hat, nor the waterproof
cape. As for the cage which the woman, who had no
other luggage, swung in her right hand, and at times
raised up to her chest, this they simply couldn't understand.

The woman was hardly four or five paces from
them when Mother glimpsed the outline of a porter
behind her, carrying the brown canvas suitcase, bulging at both sides. Then she saw the wicker travel
basket too, bound with packing twine, and the flask,
the water flask, and, on the porter's shoulder, the
white striped woollen blanket. Yes, yes, yes!

She cried out frantically:

'Skylark!' and, almost beside herself, rushed to embrace her daughter.

Father let out the same cry:

'Skylark!' And he too held the girl in his arms.

But while they were thus united, abandoning themselves entirely to their delight, a third voice called out too, farther off in the darkness, a derisive, nasal echo, rather like a cat's miaow.

'Skylark!'

It was one of those mischievous urchins who, for a couple of pennies, would carry people's bags into town. He had witnessed the theatrical outburst from a freight wagon and, finding the scene thoroughly amusing, had imitated the poor couple's voices, before quickly ducking out of view.

All three of them woke with a start from the spontaneous joys of reunion. The smiles froze on their faces.

Skylark strained her eyes towards the station building, but saw no one either on the platform or on the track. She thought she must have been mistaken and acted as if she hadn't heard. She walked on with her mother, who slipped her arm into hers.

Ákos trudged along behind with the porter. But more than once he glanced towards the wagon, his eyes piercing the darkness. He recognised that voice. It sounded like all the others, only more brazen and blunt. At one point he even stopped and took a few steps into the night towards it. But he soon turned back. Instead he swiped the air with his umbrella, dealing it one almighty blow, clearly meant for the insolent youth. Then he caught up with the two women.

Skylark was in fine spirits, witty and jovial.

'My dear parents aren't even pleased to see me. Well, well, they don't even recognise their own daughter.'

'Of course we do,' said Mother. 'It's just that hat.'

'Doesn't it suit me?'

'Yes. Only it's so unfamiliar.'

'It's a bit on the tight side. It flattens my hair,' she said, straightening her hair with her free hand. 'It's from Aunt Etelka. The cape too. So that I shouldn't get drenched.'

'It's a lovely cape.'

'Isn't it just?'

'Yes. Only it makes you different. So interesting. So independent.'

'Aunt Etelka said so, too.'

'And this?'

'Oh, yes. The cage.'

'What is it?'

'A pigeon.'

They reached the exit. Skylark again raised the cage to her heart and, while Ákos handed her ticket to the inspector, who was more than ready to go home, she coddled and cossetted her darling bird.

'Tubi. He's called Tubica. I won't let anyone take my Tubica. I'm taking my Tubica home myself.'

Outside the station, Father wanted to flag down a hackney carriage. But Skylark caught his arm and wouldn't let him. The unnecessary expense. Besides, the walk would do them good after so much sitting. The porter could carry the luggage.

Ákos gave the man the umbrella. From beneath his heavy load, the porter kept peering back to see how far they had fallen behind.

It was no longer raining and the wind had died down. Only occasional drops shuddered down from the branches of the acacias by the side of the road.

They ambled slowly on between rows of poplars.

Skylark walked in the middle, Mother and Father on either side. Father carried the flask, in which water still slopped to and fro, and the white striped woollen blanket. He gazed at the ground, lost in thought, and didn't hear a word his wife and daughter said. Again he tugged nervously at his left shoulder, carrying his invisible burden, of which he had spoken for the first time the day before. His face was affable, all the same, and he was visibly pleased by the reunion.

'So, what news?' Skylark asked her mother.

'Oh, nothing really. We were waiting for you, that's all. We missed you very much.'

They arrived at Széchenyi Square, whose usually dusty air had been swept clean by the rain. The houses stood side by side in speechless rows, curtains drawn, shutters and windows closed, looking more dwarfish than ever in the dwarfish night.

By now everyone was fast asleep. Bálint Környey slept, Priboczay slept, along with his plump wife and four exuberant rosebud daughters; Szunyogh slept, as did Mályvády, Zányi and Szolyvay; Judge Doba slept, in silence beside his lean, dark, wicked wife; Feri Füzes slept, still the perfect gentleman, smiling sweetly in his dreams, and all the other Panthers and good citizens of Sárszeg slept, including Mr Weisz, in a comfortable brass bed, and perhaps his partner too, albeit in a rather less comfortable brass bed, to be sure.

The Gentlemen's Club, whose first-floor windows would otherwise glow like banners of fire throughout the Sárszeg night, stood in mourning after the exploits of a Thursday night. Only from one window came a pale glimmer of light.

Here Sárcsevits, Sárszeg's guardian spirit, kept vigil beside an electric light, reading *Le Figaro* and advancing with the cultivated West, the enlightened peoples of Europe, on the relentless road to progress.

And someone else was still awake, too: Miklós Ijas, assistant editor of the *Sárszeg Gazette*.

After the theatre he had accompanied Margit Lator to her door, the actress to whom he was bound by such ephemeral ties as may properly bind a young, provincial poet to his muse. Sometimes he'd rest his head in her lap as she showered his chestnut mane with kisses before turning to his brow and lips. Now they had just had tea in the 'mystical half-light' cast by the little blue lamp in the soubrette's single room, which she rented for five forints a month. Both of them dreamed endlessly of Budapest, and this drew them together. On such evenings as these, Ijas would rehearse the material of his reviews, praising Margit Lator's outstanding vocal range and maligning Olga Orosz. The woman – who, incidentally, was Papa Fehér's mistress, or rather the mistress of the Sárszeg

Agricultural Bank – for her part listened patiently to Ijas's unpublished poems, which would remain in manuscript for many years to come. In a word, she appreciated him.

After this session, Ijas called in at the Széchenyi Café, where, since there was no music tonight, they were already putting out the lamps. He sat down at one of the dimly lit marble tables near the counter. As usual he ordered rum with his black coffee and smoked one cigarette after another. From the waiter's hand he snatched the latest number of József Kiss's fashionable literary journal, *The Week*, and thumbed it from cover to cover in search of the poem he had sent in months before, but always sought in vain. In his mind he dramatised this minor literary disappointment into a more general and deeply rooted *fin-de-siècle* melancholy, and, with an expression that said as much, he gazed out on the street. It was then he saw the Vajkays strolling past in a threesome, the station porter struggling on ahead.

He rose slowly and, carefully avoiding being seen, watched them with a knitted, darkening brow from behind the liqueur bottles on the counter. He even stooped a little to follow them with his gaze until they finally disappeared from view. At once he took out his notebook. Without returning to his seat, he scribbled something down, something important that he should never allow himself to forget.

'Poor Skylark with her parents walking after midnight. Széchenyi Street. Porter.'

He put the notebook back into his pocket. But then

he took it out again and stared long and hard at what he'd written, deep in thought.

Snatching up his pencil again, he added three thick exclamation marks.

The Vajkays were already passing the King of Hungary, from which the pungent smell of roast meat wafted. Skylark grimaced.

'Ugh, that awful restaurant smell!'

'We had our share of that,' said Mother with tactful contempt.

'Poor things.'

A horse and cart stood before the St Mary Pharmacy, a peasant with a large leather satchel sitting up on the box. He had driven in from his farm that afternoon to order some medication for his horse, and was waiting for the assistant pharmacist, who worked by candlelight, to finish mixing the three or four pounds of ointment in a marble mortar. Further on, the Baross Café tried in vain to attract the citizens of Sárszeg with its waterlogged, abandoned patio garden. János Csinos gave a first-rate rendition of the latest songs from *The Geisha* and *Shulamit* to empty tables and chairs.

'Did you have rain too?' asked Mother.

'Only this afternoon. The morning was lovely. We walked over to the church in Tarkő. For Mass.'

'Is today a high day?'

'Yes,' said Skylark, 'the Nativity of the Blessed Virgin.'

On the Nativity of the Blessed Virgin the swallows gather and fly to warmer climes, to Africa. All that follows then is an indian summer.

They had reached the park. Their steps echoed on the asphalt. They looked through the fence.

In the middle of the lawn, dying roses with burnt-out pistils collapsed against whitewashed posts decorated with glass balls. A light breeze scurried down the dark pathways, rattling the odd dry leaf as it passed. The benches, among them the one on which Ákos had sunned himself that Tuesday afternoon, now dripped with moisture. The lawn was turning bald. The park was deserted. Only a policeman paced up and down before the fence, greeting Ákos with a stiff salute. It was the dead of night.

Ákos gathered his nut-brown coat about him, feeling the cold. He could hear something rustle overhead, way up above in the sky.

That's the autumn, he thought to himself.

How suddenly it had arrived! Without majesty, calamity or ceremony; without carpets of golden leaves or wreaths of mellow fruit. A small, quiet autumn; an insiduous, tenebrous Sárszeg autumn.

It crouched darkly in motionless bushes, above the trees, on the rooftops. At the other end of town a train whistled, then whistled no more. A desolate boredom settled over everything. The warm days were over.

And that was all.

'There could still be some good weather to come.'

'Maybe,' said Mother.

'Maybe,' repeated Father.

At the corner of Petőfi Street they quickened their step, anxious to reach the house. Skylark had found it hard to get used to life on the plain, and not a day had passed without her longing to be home again. And now she was glad to be back in the town, which, with all its comforts, allowed people to forget so much, and held a promise of real solitude to those who had to be alone.

She could hardly wait to walk through the front door.

XIII

---

in which, on the eighth of September 1899, the novel is concluded, without coming to an end

Inside, Mother clasped her daughter in a passionate embrace.

'And now,' she said, 'I'm going to kiss my little girl to smithereens.'

Slip-slap-slop smacked the kisses.

'Stand over here,' Mother commanded, with a certain old-womanly, almost military authority. 'Stand up straight. Let's have a good look at you. Why, you're in excellent colour.'

Skylark took off her rain hat and waterproof cape.

She had indeed put on weight from all the milk, sour cream and butter. Her mouth smelled of milk, her hair of sour cream, her clothes of butter.

But the extra pounds did nothing to enhance her appearance. She had spots on her nose, thick rolls of flesh on her bosom, and her neck seemed longer and thinner than ever.

'Welcome home, my girl,' said Father, who liked to

do these things properly, and had waited for Skylark to sit herself down comfortably before greeting her thus. 'Thank heavens you're back.'

He too kissed her on both cheeks.

Clip-clap-clop clattered still more kisses.

'Oh!' cried Skylark. 'I left it outside.'

'What?'

She came back in with the cage.

'Look, isn't he sweet? Tubi. Tubica. My dear little Tubica. Isn't he a darling?'

Seeing the electric light, the pigeon began scratching with its twisted, sooty feet, turning its stupid, harmless head and blinking at its new mistress with black peppercorn eyes.

'He's quite tame,' said Skylark, opening the door of the cage. 'He'll sit on my shoulder. He always does.'

It wasn't a pretty pigeon. It was a tatty, dishevelled little bird.

'And I've got some wheat grain for you, haven't I? Where are my bags?'

Father opened the brown canvas suitcase and the wicker basket into which Skylark had packed everything so neatly, just as he had done a week before: toothbrush and comb in the same tissue paper, shoes in the same newspaper. It was from him she had inherited her love of order.

The tiny grains of wheat lay shrivelled at the bottom of a newspaper funnel fashioned from a page of the *Sárszeg Gazette*. It was the front page of the Sunday edition, and there in the middle was Miklós Ijas's poem. They fed the pigeon for some minutes, before transporting him in his wire prison to Skylark's table.

'And that's not all I've brought,' said Skylark.

The relations had sent two jars of raspberry jam, two bottles of greengage compote, a whole pork brawn and a splendid cake, in the baking of which Skylark and Aunt Etelka had quite excelled themselves.

It was a coffee-cream sponge, the type they always called 'family', or 'Bozsó', cake. It had been crushed a little by the clothes during the journey, and the filling had oozed out at the sides and smeared the paper. They all observed it for some time, shaking their heads in regret. But they managed to scrape the filling off with a knife, and it was really rather good eaten like that.

While unpacking, Skylark fished out a photograph from between her blouses.

'Guess who!' she said with a giggle, handing it to her mother.

It had been taken by Uncle Béla, who was a keen amateur photographer. Everyone was on it, including Tiger, who sat there proud and stately like a true gun dog, dangling her mammiferous belly, which was so full of gunshot from all the years of hunting that it rattled. So much so, indeed, that Uncle Béla would often wittily remark that Tiger was a veritable dog of iron.

It was a proper group portrait, comprising all the summer guests at Tarkő.

In the foreground, arm in arm, stood the two corsetless Thurzó girls, Zelma and Klári, with hairstyles *à la*

Secession and tennis rackets in their hands. Beside
Zelma stood a polished but rather irresolute-looking
Feri Olcsvay, who, poor fellow, still didn't know
whether he belonged to the Kisvárad or Nagyvárad
branch of his family.

Next to Klári knelt cousin Berci on one knee in a
mock-heroic lover's pose, leaving a visible snigger on
the faces of the two girls, who were hardly able to
suppress their giggles.

In the background, also arm in arm, stood Skylark
and Aunt Etelka.

'It's a very good photograph,' said Mother. 'Those
must be the Thurzó girls.'

'Yes.'

'The big one doesn't look very nice. The little one's
a bonny creature, but her face is so expressionless.'

Ákos asked to see the photograph. He only looked
at his daughter.

She stood by the door of the barn, which was prop-
ped open by a wooden rake. With one arm clinging to
Aunt Etelka and the other planted against the wall of
the barn, she appeared to be reaching out for protec-
tion from something that frightened her. She seemed
so alone among the others, even among her relatives,
her own flesh and blood. Only this gesture of hers was
visible, this gesture of desperate escape, which was, in
its own way, quite beautiful. Otherwise her face could
hardly be seen, for, as always, she hung her head and
showed the camera only her hair.

'Well, what do you think?'

'You look nice,' Father replied. 'Splendid.'

Skylark had finished hanging her clothes in the wardrobe and was just shutting the door when she suddenly said:

'Oh yes, did you get my letter?'

'Indeed we did,' said Father, quick to reassure her.

'Was it frightfully painful, my poor dear, that beastly tooth of yours?' asked Mother.

'Of course not. It went away in no time. It was nothing.'

'Which one was it?'

'This one.'

Skylark stood beneath the chandelier, her mouth wide open so that her mother could see, obligingly thrusting her forefinger deep inside to point out a decayed, brown tooth, half of which was missing. The other teeth at the front were like tiny grains of rice, set a little far apart, but white and whole.

'Dear me,' said her mother, stretching up on tiptoe, for her daughter was a good deal taller than she. 'You'll have to see the dentist. You can't leave it like that.'

Ákos didn't look.

He couldn't bear to witness any form of physical suffering, illness or wound.

He only stared at his daughter's face as she opened her mouth. And there, in the electric lamplight, beneath the chandelier, he could see, still more clearly than when she had gone away a week before, that a soft but indelible ashen haze had descended over her skin, like a thin, hardly visible but none the less durable cobweb. It was age, indifferent and irreparable, which he had finally accepted on his daughter's behalf, and which no longer caused him any pain. As the three of them stood there together, they really did seem quite alike.

'So, how is everyone?' asked Mother.

'They're all very well, thank you.'

'Aunt Etelka?'

'She's fine.'

'Uncle Béla?'

'Likewise.'

'So they're all well.'

In Tarkő it had been exactly the same.

'So, how is everyone?'

'They're all very well, thank you.'

'Your mother?'

'She's fine.'

'Your father?'

'Likewise.'

'So they're all well,' they had said.

But Skylark made no mention of this. All she added was:

'They send their kindest regards.'

And, unbuttoning her blouse, she began to get ready for bed.

'So you enjoyed yourself?'

'Tremendously.'

'I can't even begin to tell you tonight,' she added. 'But tomorrow. I'll speak of nothing else all week.'

'At least you had a good rest.'

'Yes.'

'And you?' Skylark began, raising her voice a little

in mild self-reproach. 'And you, my poor things? I can imagine how awful it must have been. The food at the King of Hungary.'

'Awful,' Ákos replied with a dismissive wave of his hand.

'Actually,' said Mother, playfully affecting pride, 'your father was wined and dined by the Lord Lieutenant.'

'Really?'

Skylark cast a penetrating glance at her father.

'There's something not quite right about Father. Something I don't like. Come over here, my sweet. Let me have a good look at you.'

Father went over to her obediently. He didn't dare look his daughter in the eyes. He was frightened.

'How pale you are,' said Skylark, lowering her voice. 'And how thin! Your little hands too, how thin they've grown!'

Skylark placed her bony but none the less pleasantly feminine hands on her father's and stroked his aged wrists as if they were a child's. Then she kissed them tenderly.

'Now you're in my hands,' she said in an almost manly voice. 'Father dear, you have to put on weight. Do you understand? I'll cook for you.'

'That's true,' Mother brooded. 'What shall we cook tomorrow?'

'Something light. I've had all I can take of fatty country cooking. A caraway soup, perhaps, and meat with rice. Perhaps a little semolina. And there's the cake, too.'

'And then there's washing day to think of,' Mother mumbled. 'Next week.'

Father said good night and withdrew into his bedroom, shutting behind him the door that separated it from his daughter's room. He could hear Mother discussing all the niggling details of housekeeping with his daughter, who was already in bed. Then the conversation turned to the washerwoman and Biri Szilkuthy, who had split up with her husband.

Ákos lit the nightlight. But as its feeble glow flickered across the tray on which it stood, he suddenly turned pale and shrank back as if he had seen a ghost.

There on the edge of the tray lay a slip of paper that somehow had not been hidden away in the confusion. It was the torn, pink stub of a theatre ticket for a two-seater box in the stalls, which they had brought home by mistake and kept.

He glanced towards the door, then, after crumpling the incriminating document in the palm of his hand, tore it into tiny pieces. He went over to the white tiled stove and scattered the pieces inside. When they lit the stove for the first time – in the autumn, at the end of September or the beginning of October – it would burn to a crisp along with all the twigs and logs and other lumber they had been throwing inside all summer long.

Then he got undressed. Mother came in too, on tiptoe, quietly closing the door that separated them from Skylark.

They spoke in whispers.

'Well, have you calmed down at last?' said Mother

to Father, who lay flat as a board in bed, his head on a low pillow.

'Is she asleep?'

'Yes.'

'Poor thing. The journey tired her out.'

Mother looked at her daughter's bedroom door. Her woman's heart knew all too well that her daughter wasn't sleeping.

Skylark had just switched off the electric lamp and now lay in complete darkness. She breathed a deep sigh, as she often did, many times a day, and shut her eyes. It was the end, she felt, the end of everything.

Nothing had happened, once again, nothing. As always she had only lied and smiled and tried to please everyone. But during her week away, far from her parents, something had changed inside her, something she only became aware of now that she no longer saw the folk of Tarkő before her, nor heard the rattle of the train.

'I,' she began in her thoughts, as we all do when thinking of ourselves.

But this I was her, something, someone whose life she really lived. She was this I, in body and in soul, one with its very flesh, its memories, its past, present and future, all of which we seal into a single destiny each time we face ourselves and utter that tiny, unalterable word: 'I'.

Uncle Béla and Aunt Etelka had indeed received her warmly, but she had soon discovered that her presence was superfluous, a burden, and had tried to make herself scarce, to shrink to half her size. That was why she had even slept on the divan. But somehow it was all to no avail.

Whatever she did, whatever she said, she was always in the way – of the Thurzó girls, of Berci, and gradually, as she noticed one evening at supper, even Aunt Etelka began to find her tiresome.

They were all there in the photograph she had shown her parents.

Someone, however, had been absent.

It was Jóska Szabó, the bailiff, a coarse, squat widower in his mid-forties, who had a walrus moustache and came, at least in part, from peasant stock. On the first day he had spoken to her, had walked her home from the grange. But after that he had stayed away, avoiding her company, and whenever they came face to face, he'd cast his eyes to the ground.

Yes, even Jóska Szabó, with his three motherless children, two boys and a six-year-old daughter, Mancika, whom she so loved to sit on her knee and caress. On leaving, she had given the child a silver medallion and chain which had been a confirmation gift from Mrs Záhoczky. What a ridiculous, tactless thing to have done! The shame, the awful shame! She wouldn't say anything to her parents. No, she'd tell them she had lost it.

Her relatives had invited her back next year. She had promised to return. But no, she'd never go again. What was the point?

By then she'd be thirty-six years old. And in ten years' time? Or twenty? Her father was fifty-nine, her mother fifty-seven. Ten years, maybe not even ten.

Her parents would die. And what then, Blessed Virgin, Mother of God, what then?

Above her bed, like the plaster Jesus which hung above her parents' bed, stood an image of the Virgin Mary, rocking her large, dead child on her knees and pointing to her heart, pierced by the seven daggers of maternal pain. In days long since gone by she had listened to Skylark's childish prayers, just as the prostrate Jesus heard those of her parents. For a second she flung out her arms towards the image in a gesture of passion which, however, she immediately suppressed. Patience. Patience. There are those who suffer so much more.

Her eyes still tightly shut, she lay on her cold and barren girlhood bed, where nothing, save sleep and illness, had ever happened. She pressed the full weight of her body downwards, like a corpse into its bier. The bed was softer and wider than the divan at Tarkő, and she could spread out more comfortably, soberly reflecting on the daily round that now awaited her.

The following morning she'd rise before seven and start cooking. Risotto, without pepper or other spices, and semolina so that her poor, dear father should put on weight. In the afternoon she'd go on crocheting the yellow tablecloth, which still wasn't finished, because her relatives had refused to let her work and she had succumbed to their persuasions. And then next week was washing day.

At last she opened her eyes. Darkness hovered around her, a dense and charitable blackness. At the touch of the cool air, or perhaps of the darkness itself, in which she couldn't see a thing, her eyes suddenly filled with tears. Warm, living tears flooded her pillow as if the glass of water on her bedside table had tumbled down upon it. And now she was sobbing out loud. But she lay on her stomach and pressed her mouth to the pillow so that her parents shouldn't hear. It was an exercise she had perfected through many years of practice.

Father had still not switched off the light.

'Skylark,' he faltered, pointing to the door and beaming contentedly at his wife.

'She's flown back home,' said Mother.

'Our little bird,' added Father, 'has finally flown home.'

Notes

1. Subotica today belongs to Vojvodina, until 1990 an autonomous province of Serbia. It became part of the newly created state of Yugoslavia in 1918 at the end of the First World War. As a result of the postwar settlement (Treaty of Trianon, 1920), Hungary lost approximately two-thirds of its territory and one-third of its population to the new successor states.

2. A term invented by Robert Musil to describe the Austro-Hungarian monarchy. It was coined from the abbreviation K. u. K. or K. K. (whence *Kaka*-nia), which stood for *Kaiserlich und Königlich* (imperial and royal) and was used in reference to all the monarchy's major institutions.

3. A selection of Géza Csáth's short stories is available in English. See Géza Csáth, *Opium and other Stories*, selected with a biographical note by Marianna D. Birnbaum, translated by Jascha Kessler and Charlotte Rogers with an introduction by Angela Carter, Penguin Books, Harmondsworth, 1983.

4. In addition to *Skylark*, two other novels by Kosztolányi are available in English translation: *Nero, the Bloody Poet*, translated by George Szirtes as *Darker Muses, The Poet Nero*, Corvina, Budapest, 1990, and *Anna Édes*, translated by George Szirtes, Quartet Books, London, 1991.

Central European Classics

This series presents nineteenth- and twentieth-century fiction from Central Europe. Introductions by leading contemporary Central European writers explain why the chosen titles have become classics in their own countries. New or newly revised English translations ensure that the writing can be appreciated by readers here and now.

The selection of titles is the result of extensive discussion with critics, writers and scholars in the field. However, it can not and does not aim to be comprehensive. Many books highly prized in their own countries are too difficult, specific or allusive to work in translation. Much good modern Central European fiction is already available. Thus, for example, the contemporary Czech novelists Kundera, Hrabal, Klíma and Škvorecký can all be read in English. Could one as easily name four well-known French, Dutch or Spanish novelists?

Yet, if one reaches back a little further into the past, one finds that it is the Central European literature written in German which has been most translated – whether Kafka, Musil or Joseph Roth. We therefore start this series with books originally written in Czech, Hungarian and Polish.

The Central European Classics were originally conceived and sponsored by the Central and East European Publishing Project. A charity based in Oxford, the Project worked to reduce the cultural and intellectual division of Europe by supporting independent, quality publishing of both books and journals in Central and Eastern Europe, and translations from, into and between the languages of Central and Eastern Europe. Sally Laird was Project Director at the inception of the series, and contributed much to its design. The publication of the classics is now being carried forward by the Central European Classics Trust. Besides the General Editor, its trustees are Neal Ascherson, Ralf Dahrendorf, Craig Raine and Elizabeth Winter, and the Secretary to the trustees is Danuta Garton Ash.

We hope each book can be enjoyed in its own right, as literature in English. But we also hope the series may contribute to a deeper understanding of the culture and history of countries which, since the opening of the iron curtain, have been coming closer to us in many other ways.

Timothy Garton Ash